ISBN 978-0-9862487-9-5



Published by Purple Sage Entertainment, Hopkinsville, Kentucky



W.W.Brock
brock@wwbrock.com
http://www.wwbrock.com

First Edition

# LEGION

BY

## W.W.BROCK

W.W.BROCK

# LEGION

When he opened his eyes slowly, the first thought was that he had gone blind. Darkness had set in, and the only light was from the full moon peeking dimly through the canopy of trees.

"Tommy, Tommy," a man's voice gently called to him from the dark.

"Who are you?" Tom could only see the man's bare feet and overall legs in the dark.

"Tommy, it's me, Jeremiah. We used to play together," the man answered.

"Jeremiah? Jeremiah? I remember a boy by that name many years ago," Tom's mind was fuzzy from the blow to his head.

"It's me, Tommy. You need to get up now, he's coming," Jeremiah responded.

"Who's coming?" Tom answered, still not understanding what was happening.

"He is, now let me help you up. You need to shinny this tree and wait until morning before you come down," the man answered.

Tom struggled to his feet, but couldn't seem to orient himself. A strong hand took hold on the back of his arm and guided him to a large tree with low hanging limbs.

"Grab a holt of that branch, Tommy. I'll boost you up. Get up there a ways and just hold onto the trunk until morning. He can't climb so you'll be safe until then," Jeremiah helped him up, and then vanished into the night much the same way that Tom recalled him leaving when they had finished playing that day almost forty years before.

LEGION

W.W.BROCK

# DEDICATION

I would like to dedicate this book to my wife, the love of my life. Without her support and encouragement, I would not have started writing.

W.W.BROCK

## CHAPTER 1

*"And Jesus asked him, saying, What is thy name? And he said, Legion: because many devils were entered into him."* (Luke 8:30 KJV)

The full moon flooded erratically through a veil of fast moving clouds, illuminating the dark mountainside with a cold half-light that broke through the sparse holes in the dense overhead canopy of branches covering Cannon Creek Road, the only road access to the Cannon Creek Lake landing. In the dark of the hot June night, a multitude of insects swarmed around the terrified young girl as she walked alone up the isolated trail that she had so recently traveled down with her new boyfriend, Jimmy Johnson, in his hot-rod 1956 Chevy step side pickup, complete with a custom, three hundred and fifty horsepower, three fifty Chevy motor that his daddy had built for him.

Jimmy was a real catch for a young girl like Emily Hobbs, a pretty fifteen-year-old who lived with her mother on the outskirts of Clear Creek Springs since her father had left in a drunken rage for Knoxville, Tennessee and never returned almost two years previous. An only son, and spoiled since birth, Jimmy had gotten pretty much everything in his young life that he wanted, including local athletic fame, fast cars, and any girl that he chose to wrap his arms around. Emily had been the latest of his pursuits, and tonight was supposed to be the culmination of two weeks effort on his part to add her to his list of conquests.

The Johnsons were considered to be an upper-middle class family in the Pineville, Kentucky community with their money coming from at least two generations of inheritance to Mrs. Johnson from her politically influential family that lived in Lexington. In order to keep up the appearance that he was the source of the family's prosperity, Jimmy's father owned and operated a small garage and used car dealership in Pineville, kept involved in the local politics of the community, and was largely ignored by the real movers and shakers of the area.

Emily couldn't control the trembling that her body was experiencing. It wasn't the sort of thing that came from being cold, but it was from anger and fear that she shivered as she picked up her pace on the dark roadway. To her mind, every shadow seemed to hide some malevolent creature, and she welcomed the brief moments when the moon would break through with its cold luminescence. It had been her bad luck to have left her purse and cell phone in the truck when an infuriated Jimmy Johnson, after two hours of passionate kissing, but nothing else, had issued his ultimatum, "Put out or get out!" before reaching across her and pushing open the passenger door of the truck. She laughed through her tears at the thought of bad luck. Her bad luck had been meeting Jimmy, to begin with!

Emily continued to walk the winding road until she had covered a little over a quarter of a mile when suddenly she was able to make out an area about two hundred feet in front of her that seemed to be more open. The moon came back from behind a cloud, and she thought that she could make out an object pulled off of the road in the small clearing. It was Jimmy's truck! He hadn't left her after all!

Emily started running toward the truck that was sitting with its lights off, the hood up, and the driver's door standing open.

"Jimmy!" she shouted, "Jimmy!"

There was no answer. Emily stopped running and walked slowly up to the truck, stopping at the tailgate to look around. Seeing no one, she eased along the driver's side to the open door and looked in. Her purse was still on the seat where she had left it. Emily retrieved her phone from the purse and walked to the front of the truck. Jimmy was nowhere in sight, but the smell of engine coolant was strong, and there was a dark puddle under the front bumper.

Behind her, on the edge of the woods near a pile of old timber, Emily heard a noise that sounded like a stick breaking.

"Jimmy, is that you?" she asked in an almost whisper with the question sticking in her throat.

From the darkness across the clearing there suddenly appeared to be a set of glowing red eyes staring at her, and her feet almost froze to the ground in terror.

Emily knew that Jimmy wasn't there, but she was certainly not alone. She sprinted to the cab of the truck and jumped in, pulling the door shut behind her just as something slammed into the driver side door hard enough to shake the sturdy vehicle.

Emily pushed the door handles on both doors down to lock them and then cowered under the steering wheel while she made the call to her mother for help.

"Emily Hobbs, it is after two in the morning! Where in the world have you been?" her mother's angry voice shouted in her ear.

"Mom, Jimmy, and I came to the old lake access, and he threw me out of his truck. I've been walking for a quarter of a mile," Emily responded.

"Where are you now?" Doris Hobbs asked, the anger in her voice being replaced with motherly concern.

"I found Jimmy's truck in that clear spot close to George Tuttle road. He is not anywhere around, but something is out here with me. Mom, I am so scared!" Emily answered in a frightened voice, "I've locked myself in the cab of his truck, but something is making it shake."

"Now listen to me, Emily. I'm going to get some help and come out there to get you. Whatever you do, do not open that truck door. Do you understand me?" her mom said.

"Yes, Ma'am. Mom, I'm scared, can you stay on the phone with me?" she replied.

"I'll call you right back, just as soon as I'm in the car," was the response.

Emily sat in the dark listening to the sounds of the forest. Most of the things that she heard, she knew from her father who had taken them camping almost every year since she could remember, but there was something else now that made the hair on her neck stand up.

## CHAPTER 2

"Boy, this place is bigger than I remember, Angie. I wonder if any of the old folks are still around?" Tom Strongbow said to his wife when they pulled up in the front of the First Baptist Church for Sunday service.

"We'll know in a minute, Tom. I just know that I'm here with the best-looking stranger in town!" Angie laughed as she stepped out of the truck cab and headed for the church entrance.

"Milt, look over there. Isn't that little Tommy Strongbow with that young lady?" Agnes Bunch asked the older gentleman that was standing next to her outside of the church in a group of about twenty parishioners.

"Well, I wouldn't call him little anymore, Agnes. It looks like Tommy has grown up to look like his grandfather," Milton Bunch replied.

As the heads of the group turned toward Tom and Angie, and the tongues began wagging, Sheriff Daniel Ellis pulled up to the church with the lights flashing on his patrol car. He gave a short blast on the siren to gather the crowd's attention and then made his way to the small front porch.

He shook hands with Pastor Timothy who came out of the vestibule to see what the commotion was about.

"Folks, if I could have your attention for just a minute. The Johnson boy, Ruth Ann's son, went missing last night down on the old lake road, and I need some volunteers with a little woods experience to join a search party," he said.

"Tom, it looks like he is calling you," Angie squeezed her husband's arm.

"What about church and the day we were going to spend together, Angie? This is your first trip up here, and I wanted to make the most of it with you," Tom replied, "besides, I'm in slacks and my boat shoes."

"How long could this take, Tom? The boy probably got drunk and wandered off. You'll have him back in no time," she told him with a big smile, "Besides; we've got two more days here away from the children. There is plenty of time."

Tom gave his wife a big hug and kissed her on the forehead before walking over to the Sheriff's car with six other men, one of whom looked surprisingly familiar.

"Officer Pike, I think we met in Myrtle Beach about three years ago when those cougars were terrorizing the swamp," Tom shook Bob Pike's hand as the older man struggled for a second with the memory.

"I remember now," He said, "you ran that hunting lodge up on the Pee Dee. Tom Strongbow, isn't it?"

"Yes, sir, I remember the relief when the second cat was finally taken out of the habitat. I heard about your partner. That was some bad business," Tom replied.

"Yes, it was. I'm no longer in South Carolina though. My wife and I were called to pastor a small mission in Honduras, and we came up here for her mother's funeral slash family reunion," Bob paused briefly then changed the subject, "Where is this lake that the Sheriff is talking about?"

"You see that mountain ridge behind us? The lake is on the other side, and the terrain is pretty rugged," Tom told him.

"I'm not exactly dressed for this, plus being a little old and out of shape for rugged, Tom. Maybe this won't take too long," he responded with a grimace just as the Sheriff walked up.

"Men, I want to thank you for volunteering in this search. My deputies and the wildlife folks will be up there so we probably will have plenty of armament, but if any of you want to tote a piece, feel invited to do so," he told them as his eyes scanned to small group, stopping on Tom Strongbow, "Tommy Strongbow, it's good to see you after all this time!"

"Hi Daniel, I would never have figured you for being the Sheriff twenty years ago," Tom said with a laugh as the two men shook hands, "Daniel, this is an acquaintance from the Myrtle Beach area and a former game warden, Bob Pike."

"Welcome, Bob. I'm glad to have you along because this is a really sticky situation," he replied, "A pack of hogs appears to have wiped out any evidence around the Johnson boy's truck so having a couple of professionals along will help considerably. We've got divers searching the lake, but there is so much old debris in the water that we can't drag for a body."

The men made their way to individual vehicles and Bob decided to ride with Tom since his rental wasn't exactly equipped for off-road driving.

Before leaving, Tom walked over to Angie who was busy fending off all of the town gossips and their questions, "I'm sorry about this small town stuff, Angie and I'll make it up to you when we get back, I promise."

"I'm going to hold you to it, too. Now get out of here, I'm enjoying all of the attention from your old girlfriends," she said with a laugh.

"Do you know the area where we are going, Tom?" Bob asked as they followed the sheriff's vehicle up Pine Mountain toward the Cannon Creek Lake.

"I haven't been here since the lake was built, but my dad and I hunted over there when I was a teenager," he replied, "It is pretty steep in places, and not developed much, so the kid could have just gotten turned around and walked further away from civilization. There has been talk of lost silver mines on Pine Mountain since the seventeen hundreds when a man named Swift used to bring mule trains up here to haul his silver out. At least that is the legend for this area. He could have been anywhere within about three hundred miles."

"Abigail told me stories of Cherokee mines that were supposed to be around here, but she says that nobody ever found anything," Bob told him.

"Well, with all of the coal that's been dug out of these mountains, somebody would have found it if it was here," Tom replied.

"Probably so, but you have to admit, it makes for a good story," Bob laughed.

"Well, there is some basis in truth for those legends. My ancestors on Mom's side, the Cherokee, had a chief way back that was supposed to have said that if the white man knew how much silver was in the mountains here, he wouldn't use iron to shoe his horses," Tom told him.

They drove down 25E until the sheriff turned onto Lake Hill Road and then on to the Cannon Creek Road for about a mile. At the end of that narrow road was an unmaintained boat landing that was the only access on this end of the reservoir except through the water treatment plant which was chained off. Sheriff Ellis pulled up behind one of his deputies vehicles and motioned for everyone else to do the same.

Once all of the men had assembled at the intersection with George Tuttle Road where the search command center had been set up, Sheriff Ellis gave them their orders, "Okay men, down the trail here about two hundred yards is where Jimmy Johnson's truck is sitting. I want you all to be very careful not to mess up any tracks on the road, but mark every possible sign of the boy with one of the yellow evidence flags that my deputies are handing out. Those of you with firearms, I want them carried with an empty chamber. Except for signaling, you should not have a need to use them. Do I make myself clear?"

The deputies gathered the men in groups of two men each and gave them the flags which were to be stuck in the ground wherever something was found. Tom and Bob walked behind the rest of the group with Sheriff Ellis.

"Tom, how about you and Bob work a circle about fifty yards around the truck, there hasn't been any activity in the woods yet so you might find some tracks that everybody else would miss," the sheriff told them.

"Sounds like a plan, Daniel," Tom replied, "Are you going to be at the reunion tomorrow night?"

"I had planned on it, but unless we find the boy, it might be doubtful."

"We'll find him if he is still up here," Tom reassured him, "Come on, Bob, let's see if you've forgotten anything in the past couple of years."

"Lead the way, Tom. I'll keep up as best I can," Bob said, "but I would like to look at the truck if that would be possible, Sheriff."

Daniel led the way down the trail to where the truck was sitting with the driver's door open and severely dented. The paint had been scratched to the body filler on the lower door edge with what appeared to be a sharp instrument, and the left front tire appeared to have been slashed.

"What do you think, Mr. Pike?" Daniel asked.

"From the height of the impact, I would say that you either have a cow with tusks or a large hog on the loose," Bob replied, "What do you think, Tom?"

"I'd have to agree, but when did hogs show up here, Daniel? There weren't any when we were kids that I recall," he replied.

"About nineteen and eighty eight as near as anyone can tell. That's when the first feral hogs showed up over in McCreary County. We see more and more sign every year, but this is the first time that I can recall an attack. The wildlife folks will be up here looking around today. Maybe they will have some answers," the sheriff replied.

"Well, we'll head on up the hill for a little way and see if the boy went that way," Tom said as he and Bob headed away from the rest of the search party.

When they had moved about fifty yards into the wood line, the two men separated with about twenty feet between them and started checking the ground between them for any sign of the missing Jimmy Johnson; making a circle that would take them around the truck at a distance. They could hear the other searchers downhill from them, but the vegetation was thick enough that it seemed like they were alone.

Suddenly, something glinting in the sunlight that was shining into a small clearing caught Bob's eye, "Tom, over here. I think there is something metallic on the ground!"

"What is it, Bob?" Tom asked as he walked over to the area that Bob was now in.

"Lots of pig crap, but there is something shiny in a pile of it," he replied.

Tom pulled his pocket knife out and gently moved the silver object out of the pile so they could look at it closer, "Well I'll be; it's a class ring!"

"It doesn't take a scholar to figure out how that ring got into the dung, but it also couldn't be the boy's if he just disappeared last night," Bob said.

"Well, let's flag this spot, and we'll give the ring to the sheriff," Tom suggested.

"It looks like this is a large 'sounder' of hogs. Some of these tracks look like they might belong to a three hundred pounder, but look at this one over here," Bob added as he looked around the rooted out area, "I'll bet that this is the one that rammed the truck."

"Holy Cow, that thing must be well over a thousand pounds to leave a track like that!" Tom exclaimed as he examined the print, "All of a sudden, I don't feel like being here without a firearm."

"I'm having the same thoughts, let's go," Bob agreed and they headed toward the other men.

Tom had stuck a stick into the ring to hold it until they could get it cleaned, and he handed that to Sheriff Ellis when they reached the truck.

"I don't know who this belongs to, Daniel, but it couldn't bode well for the wearer," Tom told him, "We also found some tracks up there that are bigger than any hog tracks that either of us has seen on or off the farm.”

“Good work men! I’ll give this to one of the deputies to take back to Pineville. The county has a pretty good lab there. They might be able to tell us where this came from. I think that we need to curtail this search until tomorrow in light of this discovery. We’ll see if I can’t get more men up here and some arms for you fellows.” the sheriff told them.

Bob and Tom walked back to the truck and headed back to Pineville.

“Hey, Bob, If you and your wife aren’t tied up tonight, maybe we could get together for dinner,” Tom suggested.

“I’ll have to get back with you on that. Abigail is hanging out with her family because the funeral is tomorrow. She might be ready for a break, though. The Lord knows that I am,” Bob answered with a laugh.

Tom handed him his phone number, “Give me a call if she wants to get an early dinner.”

Later that afternoon, Tom, Angie, Bob, and Abigail were enjoying the relaxed atmosphere of the Flocoe Restaurant after eating. While the two ladies made a trip to the restroom, Tom and Bob Pike talked about the disappearance and the size of the track that they had seen on the mountain. They were soon joined by a young man that had overheard a portion of their conversation.

“Excuse me, but I overheard you talking about the Johnson disappearance the other night. I wanted to tell you that the place where he went missing has a history of evil happenings and disappearances. It wasn’t too long ago that a girl was murdered down there by her boyfriend, and most of us don’t even think of going there after dark because of all the drugs and weirdness," he told them.

"Have you heard of there being big hogs in that area?" Bob asked.

"People have seen them on the lake shore from their boats, but that landing is the only access to the lake except by four wheeler, and most folks don't ride out there in the late evening anymore," he answered.

"Well, thanks for coming by and sharing that with us," Tom told him, "If you think of anything else, you should tell Sheriff Ellis."

"Sheriff Ellis already knows about the lake," the boy stated matter-of-factly, "he doesn't want people stirring stuff up about what goes on up there...says it calls too much attention to the area. Have a good night."

Tom just watched him for a few seconds as he walked out of the restaurant, "That was a peculiar thing to say about Daniel."

"I was thinking the same thing," Bob answered, "You don't think that Sheriff Ellis is trying to hide something up there, do you?"

"I've been gone a long time, Bob. Anything is possible," he answered.

The talk turned back to the hog sign that they had found that morning.

"Tom, you know that a hog can be a dangerous animal, especially when they are cornered. I'd hate to come up on anything as big as the one that made those tracks unless I had a large caliber rifle on me," Bob told him.

"I've been in some interesting situations with fair sized wounded hogs on the property, but the largest that I've seen was about six hundred give or take, and it didn't have a track with that depth. I've heard that some of the bigger hogs are taking sheep and deer when they can, and there are stories about them eating folks in east Texas," Tom told him, "I've got my Mossberg shotgun in the truck and my 1911, but neither one of them would stop even a medium hog that was ginned up. I saw Milton and Agnes Bunch before we left with the search team. If I remember, Mr. Bunch was quite the big game hunter back in the day. I'll bet that he has something that would stop elephant!"

"It's too late to ask him tonight, and you'll be in the woods at first light so better take that shotgun," Bob suggested.

"Good point, although I only packed some four aught buck this trip. Looks like it's time for a midnight Wal-Mart run for slugs," Tom replied.

"Do you think that those hogs ate that kid?" Bob asked, "Finding that ring kind of puts a damper on him being alive even if it belongs to someone else. Once they get started on a taste of 'long pig' they won't pass up another opportunity."

"Well, that's a sad thought to end the evening, but I'm leaning toward us not finding the Johnson boy. We are going back up there in the morning. Our shindig doesn't start until five or so. What time is the funeral?" Tom asked.

"It starts at eleven at the Brooks-Dunham Funeral Home, but I won't be able to get away tomorrow at all because of the family getting together after the funeral. Give me a report when you get back. I'd like to know what they find out on the ring," Bob told him.

"Sure thing, well here come the girls, we'd probably better talk about something more wholesome," Tom laughed.

## CHAPTER 3

The next morning the men met at the Sheriff's office before daybreak. Coffee and donuts were on the hood of Daniel's car, and a dozen men were already gathered when Tom pulled up in his Ford.

"Good morning, Mister Strongbow! I was hoping that you could make it this morning. Where is your friend?" Daniel asked as he slid a box of Bavarian Crèmes across the hood to Tom.

"Bob is out for the day with the funeral, but he'll probably be available tomorrow if we don't find the boy today," Tom replied shaking his head on the donut and reaching for a coffee, "I'm dressed for the hunt today, Daniel, and I'll be carrying my shotgun, if that is all right with you."

"I think everybody is packing something after word got around about the ring. You'll pair up with John Sprague here and work the area where the ring was found and maybe uphill a bit from there." Sheriff Ellis indicated a tall thin man to Tom's right hand.

"Pleased to meet you, John," he said as he offered his hand.

John Sprague just gave his head a nod and offered a handshake like a cold limp dishrag.

Something inside of him felt odd at the meeting, and Tom felt like washing his hand after the shake, but he kept that to himself. Today would be a day to keep one eye out for the Johnson boy, and one eye on Mr. Sprague.

Tom made the drive to the search area by himself after John Sprague made an excuse about having to leave early for business of some kind. The guy had a creepy aura about him so Tom was relieved not to have to make small talk on the way up. They could exchange pleasantries later in the day if there were any to exchange.

The sky was partly cloudy and promised a shower or two before the day was over, so after grabbing his day pack and shotgun out of the truck, Tom and John Sprague headed directly for the area where Bob Pike had found the ring the day before. On the way up, Tom tried to break the ice.

"So John, what kind of work do you do?" he asked.

"I'm a part-time mortician now that the mines are shutting down. Used to work for Peabody when there was work," he replied, "now I practice my taxidermy and help out if the funeral home needs a hand. You were raised around here, weren't you?"

"Yep, we are back for a school reunion. I've got a guide business back in North and South Carolina," Tom told him, "Mortician huh, what got you interested in that line of work?"

"I've always felt closer to dead people than the living, I guess," was the simple response, "When the time came to find something else to do, it just seemed natural to do what I'd always dreamed about."

Tom felt chills running up his back as he listened to this extremely strange individual talk about his work. Fortunately, they were soon at the churned up area where Bob had found the ring so that he could separate from John Sprague by a few yards.

"Let's keep parallel to each other about twenty feet apart and move along the track of those hogs toward the top of the mountain. We are looking for anything that might indicate the Johnson boy was around here after leaving his truck," Tom explained to John Sprague.

John replied with a simple nod of his head as they started their search. The trail that the hogs had followed was well worn from what looked like years of animals using it, and it meandered slightly uphill from the road below which soon put them out of earshot of the rest of the search party. The hope that Tom had of finding a footprint that didn't belong to a pig was waning when John signaled for his attention with a whistle.

"What have you got, John?" he asked when he reached the spot where the mortician was squatting down.

Sprague was using a stick to pull something up from the dirt where it had been trampled down, "It looks like maybe a wallet, but it's in pretty bad shape."

Tom marked the spot with a yellow flag and used his Garmin GPS to take note of the co-ordinates before taking his sandwich out of the baggie in his pack and handing the baggie to John for the remains of the wallet.

"John, you'd probably better take that down to the Sheriff and get him back up here. I'll stay close and look for more sign," Tom told him.

John just nodded before heading off downhill towards the rest of the searchers.

The afternoon passed with no sign of John Sprague or Sheriff Ellis coming back to look at the area where they had found the wallet, so Tom moved in a wide circle to his left and uphill. His plan was to work back toward the area where they had started the search and possibly cut some sign of the Johnson boy away from the hog trail.

Another hour into the search and Tom stopped under a large oak on some high ground that showed more evidence that the pigs had been rooting there recently. As Tom bent to retrieve his sandwich from the day pack, a bone-jarring crunch rang through his body and he fell limply to the ground.

When he opened his eyes slowly, the first thought was that he had gone blind. Darkness had set in, and the only light was from the full moon peeking dimly through the canopy of trees.

"Tommy, Tommy," a man's voice gently called to him from the dark.

"Who are you?" Tom could only see the man's bare feet and overall legs in the dark.

"Tommy, it's me, Jeremiah. We used to play together," the man answered.

"Jeremiah? Jeremiah? I remember a boy by that name many years ago," Tom's mind was fuzzy from the blow to his head.

"It's me, Tommy. You need to get up now, he's coming," Jeremiah responded.

"Who's coming?" Tom answered, still not understanding what was happening.

"He is, now let me help you up. You need to shinny this tree and wait until morning before you come down," the man answered.

Tom struggled to his feet, but couldn't seem to orient himself. A strong hand took hold on the back of his arm and guided him to a large tree with low hanging limbs.

"Grab a holt of that branch, Tommy. I'll boost you up. Get up there a ways and just hold onto the trunk until morning. He can't climb so you'll be safe until then," Jeremiah helped him up, and then vanished into the night much the same way that Tom recalled him leaving when they had finished playing that day almost forty years before.

"Jeremiah, who is coming?" Tom called in a loud whisper, but the only sounds were the breeze blowing through the trees, and something large and heavy moving his way.

He couldn't see the ground under the tree in the dark, and the brief moonlight that filtered into the forest did little to cut the fog that his head injury was causing. What he did hear was the unmistakable grunting and rooting of a very large hog directly below him, soon followed by what seemed to be a dozen smaller animals surrounding the tree base. The grunting and popping of jaws as they sharpened their cutters told him that these hogs were working up to a fight and that he was the possible adversary that they had their hearts set on.

In the faint glow of the moon, he was able to make out a large three-branch fork in the tree just above his head so Tom carefully worked his way up as quietly as possible and settled into the fork. With the trunk at his back and two smaller limbs forming a natural chair, he was able to doze for brief periods until the sun started peeking over the hills. As dawn broke, Tom looked down and saw that the herd of pigs had moved on sometime during the night and that the area under the tree was empty of animal life, although the ground looked like it had been plowed.

His dizziness was all but gone, but the pain in his head remained, so Tom did a quick self-assessment before deciding to climb back down. Once on the ground, he managed to find his pack and cell phone that lay where he had dropped them when he lost consciousness, but there was no sign of his shotgun. That phone had been trampled and the pack torn to shreds by the pigs, so Tom headed slowly back down to where he had left his truck.

"TOM…TOM STRONGBOW!" a shout rang out as Tom reached a clearing about two hundred yards from the truck.

Down below were a dozen vehicles and twice as many men who had started moving up the mountain. In the lead was Bob Pike, the man calling for him.

"I'm here, Bob," Tom answered with a wave of his arms, "I'm okay!"

Daniel Ellis ran ahead of the men and reached Tom out of breath. "What happened to you, Tom? One minute you were in the search party and the next minute you had disappeared into thin air."

"I can't recall Daniel. Something hit me on the head and knocked me unconscious. When I came to, Jeremiah was standing over me and warning me to get up a tree. I stayed there all night," He replied.

The sheriff turned to the group of men that were trailing him and shouted for a paramedic while Bob took Tom's arm and started down the hill with him.

"You need to get that scalp wound tended to, Tom. It doesn't look too deep, but there could be a concussion. I'll call Angie and let her know that you're in one piece. Jeremiah, you say?" Bob replied.

"Yeah, I played with him once when I was about nine years old. It's funny how he looked the same, except grown up," he answered, "Did the search party turn up any leads?"

"None that you didn't see early on; although, there was another hoof- print that was almost too big to be a pig's up there near where you vanished," Daniel told him, "Get patched up. We'll talk after you get some coffee in you."

"What happened to the mortician? Did John make it out last night?" Tom asked.

"He came out at dusk to tell us that you had gone missing. That's how we knew that you'd disappeared," Daniel told him.

Well, my head is telling me that Mr. Sprague may have been the one that hit me," Tom replied, "He left me about four hours before he got back here, and that is only a thirty-minute walk!"

"Well, he did bring that wallet out with him. I'll talk to him when we get back," Daniel responded half-heartedly.

Another group of men helped Tom back to the ambulance that had come along for the search. He was feeling dizzy and very tired from the activity of last night and needed to tell Daniel something, but his mind couldn't quite wrap around what he had seen and heard in the darkness of the mountain evening.

# CHAPTER 4

In the gloom of night forest floor, the huge hog stood in the middle of a pack of twenty plus feral boars all weighing between two hundred and four hundred pounds. His immense size at just over twelve-hundred pounds of body weight was accented by the coat of dark bristles that covered the body and the tall brown mane that was standing straight up in the pre-attack position. His jaws dripped foam as he continuously popped them together to sharpen the cutter teeth that protruded over six inches from his jawbone, and his stance telegraphed his intention to kill anything that opposed him.

Tonight there was a scent in the air, not like the smell of fear and death that they would smell when trailing a frightened prey animal, but a smell that only the driving evil behind the big hog's actions could discern as a dangerous adversary, of which he had very few. Even the big bears of the region walked around him if they were unfortunate to encounter him at all.

"Jeremiah," a thought passed through his memory like a whisper that would have been foreign to the hog had he not been the vehicle of a demonic evil, "Jeremiah."

There was another scent present in the air tonight, and the thought of another human nearby caused his mane to stand straight up as he searched the air for his prey. The smaller hogs were busy tearing into a pack that had a smell of food, but the big hog focused his efforts around the base of a large oak tree where the scent disappeared.

Frustrated by the escape of his victim, the big hog turned on one of the smaller two hundred pounders and quickly killed him in a fury of rage, cutting through bones and flesh with razor-sharp tusks before tearing off chunks of meat to satisfy his hunger. After feeding on the unfortunate cousin, he led his pack to a high ground water hole where they would spend the next day wallowing.

Tom made it back to the sheriff's office just before noon, and Angie was there to meet him.

"Tom, are you all right?" she asked after giving him a hug.

"Just a knot on the head, Hon. I'm sorry that I missed the reunion and worried you," he replied.

"I'm not concerned about that reunion, Tom. I'm worried about what is going on that somebody would hit you in the head over it," Angie told him, "anyway, there is the picnic in about an hour that we can go to. The reunion was kind of boring."

"You went without me?" Tom was surprised.

"I thought you might turn up late like you do sometimes, so I went to check out your old girlfriends," Angie laughed, "The only one that I found was Tessie Applewhite, your old teacher. She said that she needed to talk to you today and was very concerned that you were up on that mountain."

"Well, you'd better get me back to the motel so I can get a shower. We wouldn't want to keep Miss Applewhite waiting," Tom answered with a smile.

The reunion luncheon turned into a long question and answer session as everyone wanted to know if there had been any word on the Johnson boy, and what had happened to Tom the night before.

Tessie Applewhite finally made it close enough to pass Angie a note that read, "We'll have tea at my home after the luncheon."

The afternoon passed slowly as Tom tried to avoid any questions and still get enough to eat at the buffet tables that had been set up. It was close to five o'clock before things had wound down enough for them to leave without being noticed and make their way to Tessie's home.

"Tommy Strongbow, you haven't changed a bit!" Tessie greeted them at the door, "I met your lovely wife yesterday at the gathering, and was somewhat concerned that you were on that mountain before I could warn you."

"Warn me about what, Miss Applewhite?" Tom asked.

"It will wait until we have some tea or coffee if you prefer. I've taken to drinking tea in my old age since it seems more refined," she told them with a laugh.

"Tea will be fine Tessie," Angie spoke up, "Let me help."

Thirty minutes later, they sat in the living room sipping tea and making some small talk when Tessie finally got around to her story.

"Tommy Strongbow, do you believe in demons?" the gray-haired old woman asked Tom quietly.

Angie and Tom exchanged glances, "Why yes, ma'am, I do."

"Good! That will make me seem less crazy than most folks around here think I am when I tell you this story. Now I am a Methodist, was born a Methodist, and I will die a Methodist, but my mind has always been open to what the bible says, not like some that I know around here," she started telling her story, "About five years back there was a real fireball of a Pentecostal preacher from Knoxville by the name of Josiah Perkins that was having meetings in a home up on that mountain. They'd get all fired up and dance around, shout, and pray in tongues. Not that I was ever there, you know; my mother would spin in her grave if she found out that I was in one of those meetings!"

"We understand Miss Applewhite, but what happened at the meeting that you didn't attend?" Tom asked with a smile.

"Well, that preacher had a man in the meeting that was a bit addled. The whole town knew that he was a mite touched, had been for years, but Preacher Perkins said that he had a demon, and he was determined to cast that thing out of him during one of his meetings. They were shouting and praying, and the meeting moved outside and further away from the house. About the time that the preacher shouted, 'COME OUT OF THIS MAN IN THE NAME OF JESUS!', a herd of wild boars came busting through the meeting place squealing and raising such a ruckus that those folks ran, tripping and falling, back into the house and left that poor addlepated boy out in the woods until someone remembered to go back out there and bring him in," she told them.

"What happened to him?" Angie asked.

"Why, you know for about a week he was just fine, almost like he was never as confused as he was, and then he started to change. First, he went back to being slow, and over the next few weeks, he went downright insane. The last that I heard, he was over in that big state hospital in Hopkinsville," she answered, "That's not all either. Preacher Perkins left for Knoxville the next day and the folks that owned that cabin in the hollor just up and moved. The one thing that everybody knows but don't talk about is the demons that they let loose in those hogs that night. It was almost just like the bible except that these didn't drown."

"That's quite a story, Miss Applewhite. I don't have much experience in the field of ministering to demoniacs, but scripturally, something like this could happen. Most church folks wouldn't believe it, though," Tom answered after the old lady told her story.

"That's why I'm telling you, Tommy. Josiah Perkins told me just before he left that if the right person showed up here, I was to tell this story, and to give him a call. I'm making that call in the morning," she told him.

Tom and Angie finished their tea and bid Tessie Applewhite goodnight. Both of them were quiet most of the way back to the hotel room.

The silence in the truck was finally broken by Angie, "Do you think that story is true, Tom?"

"It would sure explain a lot of things that just don't make sense otherwise. Whether that hog that treed me the other night and these are in the same pack, I don't know. Why would Jeremiah call a hog 'He', and why don't these folks know anything about Jeremiah?" he answered.

"We'll have to pray about this, Tom. For some reason, you are the one that Jeremiah speaks to, maybe he'll get back in touch," Angie replied, "Besides, I think we will be hearing from that Josiah Perkins tomorrow. He can probably shed some light on what is really going on."

"Until then, I'm going to pay a visit to the sheriff's office in the morning and see what they've turned up on the ring and wallet that we found. I know that we have to get back home, but I'm thinking of staying a little longer to kind of see this thing through," Tom told her, "It got personal when that mortician hit me in the head."

"Well Mr. Strongbow, I'm not leaving you out here with a pack of demonic hogs by yourself. My sister can take care of the kids for a couple of days, and then we'll go home together," Angie answered, "Besides, what a story this will make for the bible study when we get home!"

## CHAPTER 5

The old flat-bottomed wooden boat pulled slowly up to the dirt landing area where Evan Myers had launched her just before dark. He had been catfishing in a secret spot that always seemed to produce the best-sized bullheads for frying, and tonight was no exception. Since the coal industry had practically shut down, Evan relied on his fishing abilities to keep a little meat on the table and save some of his meager income from the unemployment check that he got every week. He hated to take what his daddy would have called charity, but times were tough, and the family needed to eat.

He cut the antique Johnson motor and slid the boat up on the landing before getting out at the bow with the small motor and gas tank in his hands. In the full moon, he could make out his old Ford truck right where he had left it, and walked over to put the motor in the back before backing up to retrieve his boat. With his mind occupied by the thought of cleaning the almost five-gallon bucket full of catfish before dinner, Evan didn't see the first of the hogs until it had quickly and quietly run up and slashed his hamstrings with its razor sharp tusks. His screams of pain and surprise went unheard as he tried desperately to pull himself into the truck bed with his arms, to no avail. Something had gotten hold of his right leg and was pulling him viciously down and away from the truck. The last conscious thoughts that went through his terrified brain were the glowing red eyes of a monster hog as it dragged him off into the woods and away from the lake and the fact that the others were eating him alive.

"Good morning, Tom. Are you feeling better this morning? How is the knot on the head doing?" Sheriff Ellis asked him.

"I'm fine Daniel, just wondering if you had any news on the ring or wallet yet?" Tom asked.

"No, I expect something this afternoon, though. Right now I've got another missing person to check on. Evan Myers didn't come home from fishing last night and his wife is frantic. If you aren't in a hurry to go somewhere, take a ride with me," the sheriff invited.

"I'll have to let Angie know where I'm headed. Can we get back by noon?" Tom asked, "I'm meeting Bob Pike to see what their schedule is."

"I'll make sure you're back. We can catch up in the car." Daniel told him as he walked around to the driver's side of the Ford Expedition that was the Sheriff's patrol car.

"I'm assuming that this fellow was fishing close to where the Johnson boy disappeared. Am I right?" Tom asked.

"I'm afraid so. He liked to fish in a place that he thought nobody else knew about, but it is at the end of that road that we found the boy's truck on. I've got a bad feeling about it." Daniel replied.

"Daniel, were you the sheriff when Josiah Perkins was holding his meetings up there a few years back?" Tom thought it was as good a time as any to ask.

"You mean the old demonic hog tales that came from those meetings, don't you?" Daniel answered with a laugh, "I don't believe in those things, Tom."

"So there was a preacher by that name up here then. What happened to the folks that owned the house that they held the meetings in?" Tom asked.

"Folks made so much fun of them that they packed up and left…didn't even sell the house," He responded.

Tom didn't speak any more about it after that, and they made small talk until they reached the broken pavement that led to the landing where that Myers fellow had left his truck.

"Daniel, pull up here and let me walk in front of the truck for the last hundred yards. There might be some sign if nobody else has been here," Tom told him.

"Good idea," Daniel agreed as Tom stepped out onto the broken asphalt of the road.

"How about getting a gun ready just in case, Daniel. I feel kind of naked out here," Tom said with a serious look on his face.

Daniel just nodded and pulled his service Glock to be ready. They moved slowly down the path until Tom raised a clenched fist suddenly as a signal to stop. Daniel got out and walked around to him.

"What is it, Tom?" he asked.

"Blood and a lot of it! It leads from the truck over there up through this trail to our left and uphill into the woods." Tom replied.

Daniel went back to the patrol car and radioed for one of his deputies to bring the search party down while Tom walked over to the boat. It was sunk in the shallow water with just the bow touching the landing. The bottom had been stomped out by hogs going after the fish bucket that was now lying empty on the landing.

Daniel came over to where Tom was standing and handed him his duty AR-15.

"This is a little light for hogs as big as these seem to be, Tom, but it does have a thirty round magazine."

"Thanks, Daniel. I have a very bad feeling about what is on the other end of that blood trail," Tom told him as he racked a round into the chamber of the AR.

The two men worked slowly up the hill through the tangle of undergrowth as they followed the blood trail that got weaker the further they went.

"Whatever is bleeding is about bled out," Tom said in a whisper.

They stopped where the blood trail ended abruptly and looked at every leaf and twig until Tom spotted some red on a sapling about twenty feet in front of them. They made their way slowly to the blood stain and looked for several minutes before another one was spotted further to their right hand and slightly downhill where a pile of boulders protruded from the forest floor to a height of about twenty feet.

As they cautiously and quietly approached the rock formation, Tom heard the unmistakable sound of a hog chomping his jaws and sharpening his cutters. He slipped the safety off of the AR and signaled for Daniel to keep his eyes open. Tom eased around the first boulder and spotted two large hogs in the four to five hundred pound range squaring off with each other in what appeared to be a territorial dispute. Without hesitation, he placed one round directly into the ear of the nearest hog which dropped where he was shot. The second and larger of the two did not hesitate before charging directly at the new enemy.

Tom got another shot off before climbing up the boulders to get his legs away from the cutters on this massive animal. He heard the

.45 caliber Glock of the sheriff fire twice before he turned in time to see the hog roll over once and then get back on his feet to charge Daniel. Tom led the hog's eye about two inches and began firing as fast as he could cycle the trigger until the animal rolled up a scarce two feet from where Daniel was backed up against the rocks.

"You took long enough, Strongbow. I was beginning to think that you still held a grudge over Susy Morgan," Daniel laughed.

"You did me a favor, Daniel. That's why the hog didn't get to you. Whatever happened to Susy anyway?" Tom asked.

"I married her three years ago. Both of us were on the rebound. So far it's been good," Daniel responded.

"Not that the subject matter isn't gripping, but what are you going to do with these hogs? Somebody needs to open them up for a look at the stomach contents, and I wouldn't do it up here…if you get my meaning," Tom told him.

"Agreed, the reinforcements should be at the lake by now, let's send them back up for the hogs. I'm going back to town and get a change of underwear." Daniel told him.

"I'm right behind you sheriff. We need bigger weapons when we come back," Tom responded as he followed Daniel back down the hill to the lake.

"I thought that you were leaving tomorrow, Tom. What's up?" Daniel asked.

"I just thought that this would be an experience that shouldn't be missed, and I can be of help, so we elected to stay for a couple more days." He replied.

"I'm glad to have you. Not many around here could have stopped that hog today. I'm obliged," Daniel said in a tone that made Tom think otherwise.

They made the clearing where two deputies and five others were looking over Evan's truck. Daniel sent them up to gut the hogs and bag the contents, and then he and Tom returned to Pineville.

## CHAPTER 6

Trapped inside the mind of a twelve hundred pound hog with hundreds of spirits as evil as himself, all of whom were fighting for control of the beast was taking a toll on the demon Turel, their prefect. For thousands of years, he and his tribe had been finding one host after another to control with every type of sickness, plague, and evil known to man, and had escaped being cast into the dark Pit that harbored the old ones in torment since the arch-angel Michael had thrown Azazyal in and covered him with sharp rocks by God's command millennia past. Now they were trapped in this hog that refused all of their efforts to control its movements, bringing them perilously close to their mortal enemy, the angel Raphael on several occasions. Turel thought that he had found the perfect host in the last human that they inhabited, but that meddlesome preacher had exhibited the faith that it took to call them out. It was only because of the herd of hogs running through that they were able to avoid the abyss on this one, but the alternative was to inhabit this beast until they could find another human host. Now that possibility was being diminished almost daily as the animal killed and ate all of their prospects. Turel had made up his mind that if and when they did manage to escape imprisonment in the hog,  he would exact vengeance on those responsible for casting them in here, and no corner of the earth would hide them.

When Tom arrived at The Flocoe restaurant, he was surprised to see Tessie Applewhite and a well dressed, older, white-haired gentleman in his late seventies sitting at one of the larger tables with Angie, Bob, and Abigail Pike.

"Hey folks," he greeted them while leaning over to give his wife a kiss, "Miss Applewhite, this is a pleasant surprise."

"Tommy, this is Josiah Perkins, the preacher that I told you about," she replied with a smile.

"Good to meet you, Josiah," Tom offered his hand.

"And I you, Mr. Strongbow. Tessie has filled you in on what I'm here to talk about, I take it?" he said as he shook Tom's hand.

"Yes, we had a talk with Tessie the other night, but the Pikes here have not heard the story," Tom replied.

"Good, let's eat and then I'll share what I've come to say. Quite possibly you folks can help me get the 'genie back in the bottle', so to speak," Josiah replied with a big smile.

The table conversation was mostly small talk as they ate their lunch with Josiah purposely avoiding any questions that related to the incident of five years before until after coffee and a bit of dessert. Finally, the last plate was cleared from the table and all eyes were turned to the small old man with the sparkling eyes.

"For the benefit of Bob and Abigail, I'll start at the beginning," he said, "I came up here about five years ago in hopes of building a fellowship of faith-filled believers along the lines of our full gospel ministry in Knoxville. We had several meetings out on Cannon Creek Road in the house of Emmet and Judith Sparks before I thought that there was enough faith in the group to relieve that young man, Michael, of his demons. Well, I'm not too proud to admit that I made a very serious error in not listening to God on the matter. We decided to hold that meeting outside of the house and invited Michael up for dinner and prayer. I think we took those demons by surprise though, because things really got active when we started praying for the boy's deliverance. By the time I ordered them out, I knew that I'd made a mistake because everybody except the Sparks were looking aghast at what I was doing. About the time that I called those demons out, a herd of a dozen or so hogs came crashing down the mountain and through the yard just squealing and snorting led by one huge beast, and then just as quickly went off back the way that they had come. Almost everyone ran back in the house in a panic, and I went in after them to get those folks calmed down a bit. Tessie here had the presence of mind to go back out for Michael and bring him in," Josiah related the story.

"So you think that this hog that we are looking for is part of the same herd that you encountered that night?" Tom asked.

"Yes, but there is one thing you should consider before this takes on the proportions of a bad horror film. If you recall, Jesus cast the demons out of the demoniac mentioned in Luke into a herd of hogs that then ran down into a lake and drowned. Those demons would have controlled those hogs if they could have, so I'm of the mind that they cannot control those animals up on the mountain, just possibly make them meaner and more aggressive than normal. The thing to watch for would be having an unbeliever in the group if you get the chance to cast those demons back into the abyss because they might enter an individual without Jesus inside through an open mouth, eyes, or something. I've not had any experience with animal demoniacs, only people, but they certainly can exist! Another thing is that these hogs are dangerous with or without a demon inside, and I think that you are going to have your hands full with the hogs even if they don't carry Satan's spawn with them," he finished.

Bob Pike looked at Abigail, then at Tom and Angie before speaking, "Two years ago, I would have pooh-poohed any notion that this type of thing could happen in a modern era, but after serving in Honduras, Abigail and I have seen some things that make this a pretty tame sounding venture. Speaking for myself, I want to see this through to the end. How about you, Honey?"

"I'm in too. Besides, I'm not leaving Angie here by herself with you men tramping the woods. We might have to come and bail you out," she laughed, not knowing how prophetic her statement was to be.

"I've got two extra bedrooms at my house," Tessie piped up, "You all need to pack your things and move in until all of this is taken care of. Besides, I would feel much better with company around,"

"Tessie, we wouldn't dream of imposing," Angie started.

"Nonsense, I insist on it, besides, think of all the town busybodies talking about me for a change. I haven't had that much attention since I went to Nashville forty years ago with Kurt, my second husband, for a month and came back married!" Tessie laughed, followed by a quickly added, "Sorry Pastor."

"No offense taken Miss Applewhite. Now, I'm too old to go chasing after these hogs with you men, but you wouldn't need me anyway. I feel that you are both strong enough in spirit to confront these things and to get them back in the Pit where they belong. I will be available by cell phone twenty-four hours a day until this situation is resolved, so put my number on speed dial." he told them as he stood up.

"Before you go, could you pray for us, Josiah?" Tom asked.

"I'd be happy to," Josiah gave them his benediction.

# CHAPTER 7

Sheriff Daniel Ellis sat across the large desk from someone that he had known for most of his life as a very powerful man. As a matter of fact, former Senator Andrew Trent was the man most responsible for Daniel being sheriff of Bell County so he commanded a lot of respect from the young lawman.

"Senator Trent, I understand that we have a timetable to meet, but this hog business is putting a real damper on our activities, and on our ability to sneak that silver out of the hole that it is stored in," Daniel told the man in the two thousand dollar suit.

"I don't need to tell you, Ellis that I've gone to considerable lengths to keep the treasury people off of us, not to mention the IRS, and I need that silver brought across that lake and flown out of the country by the end of the week. How you do it is up to you," the Senator told him, "My people are screaming their fool heads off now that we are two weeks behind schedule. You need to take some action immediately. Did I make myself clear?"

"Yes Sir, very clear, sir," Daniel stood to leave the man's presence, "Just one more thing Senator, I've got some people on the search party that are very perceptive. How should I handle them?"

"How have you handled the others, Ellis?" Trent just gave him a glower and went back to his paperwork that was in front of him.

Daniel just nodded and left the room with a sick feeling in his stomach. The 'others' that Trent had referred to were several drug dealers and clients that had stumbled on Daniel and his men as they brought some of their contraband to the landing late in the evening hours. Several had been lowered into the deeper areas of the lake, while some were the victims of staged overdoses and left lying near the landing as a warning to others. Now with the killer hog pack bringing unwanted media attention to the lake, the operation to smuggle out two hundred and fifty thousand silver coins from a cache that Daniel had found while hunting was in jeopardy. That meant Daniel and his wife were in jeopardy also since the people that Senator Trent represented would not hesitate to sink them in the lake with the others if this operation went awry.

Daniel's thoughts were interrupted by his cell phone ringing.

"This is Sheriff Ellis," he answered.

"Sheriff, we are at the county morgue with those hog guts. You need to come over right away," his deputy said.

"What did you find?" he asked.

"Well, there are body parts in both of them that belong to Evan Meyers, and there is a bracelet in the larger of the two with Jimmy Johnson's name on it," came the reply.

"Good work! I'll be right there," Daniel said and ended the call.

And just like that, there was a glimmer of light at the end of his tunnel.

Tom's phone rang as he was leaving the Flocoe with Angie and the Pikes, "Hello."

"Tommy, this is Daniel. I've got a breakthrough on the missing boy case and thought that you would like to tag along," Daniel told him.

"Sure, can I bring Bob Pike with me? I'm sure that he would be interested in the outcome," Tom asked him.

"Absolutely, meet me at the coroner's office on Cherry Street in five minutes," He ended the call.

That's interesting," Tom told them.

"What is?" Angie asked.

They've got something that might close this case and Daniel wants us to go with him to see it," he said referring to Bob and himself.

"You men go ahead, Angie and I will start getting our stuff moved to Tessie's," Abigail told them.

"We won't be long unless something really strange is going on. I'll call if we're not going to make it back in time to watch the sunset," Tom promised.

The two men met Sheriff Ellis outside of the medical examiner's offices and went in after him. They were introduced to Doctor Glenn Hickey, an older pathologist that had a bored look about him.

"Well, folks, let's go see what these people brought me to identify," Hickey said as he led the way to an examining room in the basement.

On the table was an assortment of small body parts, the most recognizable a finger with the wedding band intact.

"I couldn't get any of the Johnson boy's DNA from that mess, but it is almost certain that he was eaten by what the boys said was the larger of these hogs. I believe they said it was light in color," he paused to look at his note, "Yes, the larger of the two and light in color. Well, Sheriff, this should solve your case for you, but it won't bring much comfort to Ruth Ann, some closure maybe, but no comfort."

"As soon as you get the paperwork to me, I'll inform the family, Glenn," Daniel told him, "Well Tom, you folks don't have to prolong your vacation anymore. It looks like you killed the killer.

You always did have a flair for being in the right place at the right time, didn't you?"

"Wow, talk about luck. Who would have thought that you two would just stumble onto the two hogs that have been doing the killing up there," Bob laughed, "Well good work, men. I'm going to tell Abigail to get us packed when we get back."

"Daniel, I've got to admit that this was an unusual reunion for me, and I'm glad it is almost over," Tom said as he shook Daniel's hand.

"Almost?" Daniel asked.

"Yeah, we've got a couple of people to see before we leave, and Angie wanted to watch a sunset from Clinch Mountain," Tom told him.

"Oh, well okay then. If you get back in this area, give me a call, Tommy," he answered as the two men left the building.

Once outside and away from prying listening devices, Bob asked, "How much of that dog and pony show did you believe?"

"Not much, although I don't doubt that those hogs had a part in eating Meyers and the boy, Daniel was too obvious in his desire for us to leave town," Tom replied.

"Well, the game warden in me says that we might need to sneak back out there and do a little investigating on our own," Bob said.

"I've got two Spy Point trail cams in my truck that will transmit a video if we can get them set up out of sight of the sheriff," Tom told him, "I still think we need a heavy rifle, just in case. I'll call on Milton Bunch this evening and see what he might have that I can use."

"It sounds like we might have a working plan, Tom. Let's get with the girls and pray about what we are getting ready to do. I'd hate to step in front of the Lord on this," Bob said.

"Great idea and we need to head to the Clinch Mountain Restaurant if we are going to catch the sunset tonight. With a little help from the girls, we might be able to 'stealth' our way in there about one AM," Tom added, "There is something gnawing at me, though. I know that mortician hit me on the head, and I would like to ask him why before we go watch the sunset."

"Do you think that's wise, Tom? I mean, if Sheriff Ellis gets word that we are still stirring this pot and he involved in whatever is going on, he might try to stop us in a not so friendly manner," Bob told him.

"The chance of getting caught up there is pretty slim if we go in on foot. The girls can drop us off on that George Tuttle Road up from where the truck was found, and we'll hike in, hang the cameras, and hike back out. I figure about twenty minutes tops," Tom reassured him, "Do you want to come with me to find John Sprague?"

"As long as you don't do anything to get us locked up, I'm game," Bob replied half-heartedly, 'Do you know where to find him?"

"From what John told me before he hit me in the head, he's got his mother's old place out in Mudlick Holler. I know he doesn't work except when there is an overflow at the funeral home, so maybe we can catch him out there," Tom replied, "We'll pick up Angie and Abigail so we can go straight to Clinch Mountain afterwards, but first I need to make a stop at the Bunch's and see if he has a couple of rifles that we can use."

Agnes Bunch answered Tom's knock and expressed her pleasure at seeing him standing on her porch.

"Tommy Strongbow, I am so glad that you came over," she bubbled, "Milt, Milt, we've got company! Come on in Tommy and bring your friend. You must tell me what has been going on with you and that lovely wife of yours, and introduce us to your friend."

After the introduction, Agnes fussed over them as she led Tom and Bob into the living room where she insisted that they sit and partake of a cup of coffee.

"No thank you, ma'am," Bob replied, "We just stopped by to talk to your husband about his hunting days."

"Nonsense, Mr. Pike, one cup of coffee never hurt anyone, did it Tommy?" she said as she went out of the room.

Milton Bunch entered the room as his wife was heading into the kitchen. He was an impressive man in his early seventies with wide shoulders and a military bearing that spoke of the years that he spent in the Marine Corps.

"Hello Tom," he said as he shook Tom's hand.

"Hello Mr. Bunch, this is my friend, Bob Pike, an ex-game warden turned pastor," Tome replied.

"I'm pleased to meet you, Bob. That is certainly an interesting change of occupations, you have to admit," Milton told him.

"Yes sir, I suppose it is, but the circumstances behind the change were interesting also," Bob replied.

"So what did you want to know about my hunting background? I heard you talking as I was coming down," he said with a smile.

"Well, Mr. Bunch, I was wondering if you might have a couple of heavy rifles that you could loan us for two days without telling anyone?" Tom asked a bit nervously.

"If you mean tell Daniel Ellis, you should know that there are quite a few of us that know Sheriff Ellis has let some unsavory elements influence him for the past year or longer. Any business that you have with me will surely stay in my home and between us, provided that Agnes doesn't overhear," Milt told them with a smile.

"Overhear what, Dear?" Agnes came in with a tray of coffee and a few cookies.

"Just hunting talk Agnes. The boys wanted to know what type of rifles that I used on safari," he told her, "I've got two favorites. One is a pristine model 30S Remington that I had rebarreled some years ago and chambered for the .375-338 or 375 Taylor. It has about the same ballistics as the old 300 H&H, and I've never had any animal question the slight difference in bullet speed when they got hit. The other is an older Rigby side by side in .416 Rigby that is regulated at fifty yards. I've taken buffalo with both rifles and one elephant with the .416."

Agnes just rolled her eyes and excused herself from the room while the topic of hunting was being discussed so Tom seized the moment.

"Both of those would fill the bill, sir. Do you have any loads for them?"

"I've got a box or two of 300 grain Barnes solids loaded for the .375 and a box of 400 grain Barnes solids for the .416. Do you mind if I ask what you boys are planning on shooting with them?" Milt asked.

"We are going to try and kill the big hog that we believe is running that herd up by the lake," Tom told him.

"You need to be careful with those hogs, son. There are other things involved that I'm not going to speak of that might put you in jeopardy with that creature," Milt replied.

"If you mean the demons, sir, we're equipped to handle them as well," Bob reassured them.

"I'll get the guns and meet you out back. Let me go tell Agnes that you had to leave," Milt told them while ushering them quietly out of the front door.

## CHAPTER 8

The small two-story frame home that housed John Sprague sat well back in the isolation of Mudlick Holler with a solid wall of limestone at its rear. Its last flake of paint had weathered off at least a decade before exposing the sawmill slab exterior to the elements, and the porch had started rotting at the edges from rain seeping through cracked and faded deck paint. The cracked windows that Tom could see as they pulled the Ford up the dirt drive were fitted with dark curtains that looked dirty and torn from years of neglect. No one spoke a word as they sat for about five minutes just looking at the home and wanting to change their minds about going in.

"Well, I came to see this bird, so it is now or never," Tom spoke to break the silence.

"I'm going in with you, Tom, but you had better leave that pistol in the truck so we don't give the wrong impression," Bob said quietly, "Besides, he's watching you from the right hand upstairs window."

"We'll just sit out here and pray dear. You can leave the pistol with me…just in case you don't come out," Angie said nervously.

Tom just gave her a 'look' and handed the 1911 over.

"Come on Bob. These women are starting to creep me out," he said as he got out of the truck.

They walked to the rotting steps and up onto the creaking porch. Tom knocked on the door and then listened for the sound of movement inside. A dirty curtain pulled aside to his right revealing the face of John Sprague.

"John, open the door. I need to talk to you," Tom called out.

The door knob turned as Sprague slowly pulled it open with the loud squealing of a dry hinge pin.

"What do you want?" he asked nervously as he looked at the two men in the doorway.

"John, I know that you hit me in the head the other day and left me up there on that mountain for those hogs. Why did you do that, and where is my shotgun?" Tom asked.

"He made do it, I swear," the pasty looking man stammered and backed slightly into the house.

Tom took that as an invitation and followed him in.

"Who is this 'he' that I've been hearing about?" he pressed thinking that John was referring to the same person that Jeremiah had mentioned.

"Sheriff Ellis told me to make sure that you didn't come back down that mountain until late, and I done that. I swear that your shotgun was there after I hit you," Sprague babbled, "He didn't mean for you to be up there all night and was plenty sore at me for hitting you too hard."

Bob was looking around the filthy house at the piles of animal hides and mounted heads that filled almost every room. It was obvious that John Sprague liked dead animals as well as humans, and from the rotting smell that permeated the place, was not too handy with the tanning process.

"I'll bet that the Kentucky Wildlife folks would like to know about your little hobby here, John. I think that we will call them when we leave," Bob threatened him.

"I'm not doing anything wrong. They make me do these things," Sprague said in a pitched whine.

"Who makes you, John?" Bob asked.

From deep within Sprague came a deep voice, "I make him, Christian!"

Bob took over now as if his time working with the Honduran natives had specifically prepared him for this task.

"Demon, I command you in the name of our Lord, Jesus Christ to leave this man and return to the abyss!" he spoke with authority.

John fell to the floor and flopped violently with blood running from his mouth as he almost bit the end off of his tongue. Tom found a piece of wood on the dirty table and hurriedly jammed it between Sprague's teeth.

"I said to leave this man and return to the pit, Demon. DO IT NOW!" Bob spoke.

Something resembling thick smoke started out of Sprague's mouth and slithered across the floor to the open door where it disappeared into the air, and Sprague's convulsions quit as soon as it was gone.

"John, can you hear me?" Bob asked.

A weak reply came from his bloody lips, "Yes."

"John, are you ready to get your life turned around now?" Tom asked him.

The men knew that in order to keep that demon from returning with seven of his friends, John was going to have to sincerely accept Jesus into his life.

"I don't know how I'm going to do that," he replied weakly.

"Fortunately for you, we do!" a new voice spoke from the doorway.

The men turned their heads in surprise and saw Angie and Abigail coming into the house.

"Some things need a woman's touch, men. Let us pray with Mr. Sprague while you fellows take a look around," suggested Angie.

After exchanging looks, Bob and Tom walked into the back of the house to see if there was anything that would tie John Sprague to the disappearances but found nothing. After a brief search, they came back to the front room to find John Sprague sitting in a chair with his head bowed and repeating 'Amen' to the prayer of the two women.

"We are going to leave now, John. I am going to mention to Pastor Tim Swift that he should come out here and see you. Is that okay?" Tom asked.

"Yes sir, and I am sorry about hitting you in the head Tom," John said with tears in his eyes.

"That's a good start, but don't say anything to Sheriff Ellis about us being here," Tom told him as they walked out.

"I won't say anything, just be careful. There is a lot of evil in those woods," John replied.

Tom just nodded and followed the others to the truck, nervously checking every few steps to see if anything was following.

## CHAPTER 9

"I don't understand why we can't just drive up George Tuttle Road and take the four wheelers in there after that silver, Daniel. It doesn't make sense to ferry the stuff across the lake when we can drive almost all of the way in. That's all I'm sayin'," Johnny Simpson told Daniel Ellis.

"I've told you before, there are too many houses back up in those hills for us to be driving in and out, Johnny. What we are doing violates Federal law, and if we get turned in, you can kiss that money good-bye!" Ellis replied, "By the way, that was a nice touch throwing the kid's bracelet in with the hog stomach contents. It took a lot of heat off of this search."

"I did it real slick like too. Even Walt didn't see me add it to the pile," Deputy Simpson bragged.

"Okay, now I need to have you over in the cave tonight to get that silver rounded up and put into the tubs that I got for you. Anybody that sees you crossing the lake will think that you are fishing late. Just be careful of those hogs if you come out after dark. They are the one thing that we didn't count on," Daniel cautioned.

"I'll be getting there just before sunset and nobody uses the landing during the week but druggies, and that is way too early for them to be out," Simpson told him before leaving the office.

Daniel sat back in his chair and clasped his hands behind his head. Two more days and this would be over, he thought, just two more days before he and Susy could plan that vacation that they had been talking about since they met. There were still some loose ends to clean up, of course, but now that Tommy Strongbow was leaving along with his game warden friend, everything was back on track.

The sunset view from the Clinch Mountain Restaurant lookout was spectacular, just as Tom had promised everyone that it would be, but he was distracted by thinking of what they might find on the trail cameras that they had set on the way up here. The plan went off like clockwork with a mad sprint to the landing by Tom with one camera, and Bob Pike taking the other into the clear area where Johnny Johnson's truck had been found.

Now it was just killing enough time to gather the recorded data from a safe distance thanks to the remote function via cell phone, and hopefully, they would have something to take to the authorities outside of Daniel Ellis' jurisdiction.

They had just finished their meal when the patrol car of Sheriff Daniel Ellis pulled up in the parking lot.

"This can't be a coincidence, Tom," Bob said.

"We'll see, maybe he is just out for a bite to eat," Tom replied.

The two women looked nervously at their husbands while Daniel strode to the restaurant with one of his deputies and straight back to where they were sitting.

"Hello Daniel, what in the world is a Kentucky sheriff doing in Tennessee?" Tom asked as if he didn't know.

"Tommy, did you drive out to see John Sprague this afternoon?" he asked.

"Yes, I did, Sheriff. We stopped by to see if he had my shotgun," Tom responded calmly, "He didn't, so we came up here."

"John Sprague is dead, and I'm going to have to take you back in for questioning. Are you going to come quietly?" he asked as the deputy grew an evil looking grin across his face.

"You should know that John told all of us that you ordered him to knock me out, Daniel. I think that the authorities outside of Bell County would like to know what you've been up to. You know that I didn't kill John Sprague. Are you sure you want to open up this can of worms?" Tom asked, "Besides that, you don't have anything but bluff working for you here."

Daniel just stared at him and the rest of the table with anger and fear showing on his face. The deputy had worked his way around behind Bob who just sat quietly waiting to see what was going to happen.

"Look here Strongbow, I don't take kindly to being threatened, especially by you!" Daniel blustered.

"If you think that it is a threat, go ahead and take me in for questioning. There are plenty of people in Pineville that will vouch for me, and I would question whether the same can be said for you," Tom responded firmly.

"Well…just don't leave town again until we get to the bottom of this!" Daniel exploded before turning abruptly and leaving.

"Oh, you can bet we won't," Tom said under his breath.

"Abigail, I want to personally put the cuffs on that deputy," Bob said to his wife, "and we are going to stay until it is done."

Angie spoke up, "Tom, this man is deranged if he thinks that we will just roll over for him. He killed that poor man today right after we left."

"I have a hunch that the deputy did the killing. He looked like he would enjoy that sort of thing. Thank God, John made the right decision before we left him," Tom said, "Now, let's pay up and go kill some time before we check on the cameras. On second thought, let's have a look at them now just to see if we've caught anything."

Tom used his app for the camera site and soon had some streaming video of the landing and the clearing off of the Cannon Creek Lake Road. It didn't take long for them to see Deputy Simpson launch a johnboat stacked with plastic tubs, and then motor off across the lake after checking to see if anyone was looking.

The camera overlooking the clearing hadn't picked up anything except a blurred picture of the deputy's truck as he drove past to the landing. Suddenly, in the right-hand corner of the next frame, a large hairy snout showed up followed by a set of white tusks.

"Bob, how high did you set your camera?" Tom asked.

"About three feet high, Tom, why?"

"Your hog is standing next to it!" Tom exclaimed as he handed to phone to Bob.

"Boy that is a healthy beast!" Bob exclaimed and showed it to the two women.

"Well, we can't very well go down there tonight and shoot it with that deputy on the lake. Daniel will probably be right on our tail when we leave here anyway. Let's just go back to Tessie's and keep an eye on the cameras until tomorrow. Maybe something else will turn up," Tom suggested.

"Sounds like a plan. I'm a little beat from the excitement today anyway," Bob replied, seconded by Abigail.

The herd of hogs, led by the twelve hundred pound beast that also hosted the demon Turel and his troop, moved across the Cannon Lake Road and around the lake in search of the human that had recently left the landing. Their keen sense of smell picked up his scent from across the water, and the noise that he made as he unloaded his supplies tickled their ears. Running at a fast pace, the hogs made their way almost silently around the lake on a little used four wheeler trail that ran just below George Tuttle road. Within thirty minutes, the hogs had found Deputy Simpson and watched as he carried supplies into a well-hidden cave close to the lake surface. The opening would have been a couple of hundred feet above Cannon Creek before the dam was built, and any memories of its location would have faded long ago as it had not been used since the seventeen hundreds.

Sensing no danger, the hog moved quietly and quickly to get behind the man that he watched and was just about to take him when the sound of a second human came from inside of the cavern.

"Deputy Simpson, is that you?" came a voice from inside.

"Yeah, Johnny, I've got some digging tools and some grub for you," Simpson answered, "Just hold your voice down. I don't want anyone else to know we are here."

Simpson had just stepped into the cave entrance when one of the smaller hogs decided to rush him despite being low in the hierarchy of the herd. Johnny Johnson saw the attack taking place and put a well-placed shot with an old model 94 Winchester directly into the left front shoulder of the four hundred pound attacker, but not before it had cut completely through the quadricep muscle of Simpsons left leg with his razor tusks.

The hog spun around at the impact of the bullet and just as quickly turned back to attack the wounded deputy again. The next round from the rifle caught him in the eye, killing the hog immediately, but not before Simpson was a blubbering mess on the ground with both legs badly cut to the bone and bleeding profusely. Johnny quickly grabbed an old fish towel that was in the cave with his camping gear and tried to tie off the spurting blood on Simpson's left leg.

"I need the keys to your truck so we can get out of here," the Johnson boy told the deputy.

"In my right front pocket, Johnny, get me to the boat," Simpson pleaded.

Johnny helped him to his feet, but Simpson was too far gone from the loss of muscle and blood to do more than hobble, much less try to outrun a herd of hungry hogs with the scent of blood in their noses.

As they moved out of the cave mouth, the big hog drew back into the brush and waited with the others following his example even though the smell of blood had them popping their jaws and sharpening their cutters until a slobbery foam hung from their mouths.

Frustrated at the thought that this filthy hog was going to kill another perfectly good host, the demon Turel practically screamed in frustration for the hog to stop his attack, to no avail.

The two men were about halfway in their twenty-yard hobble to the boat when the hogs had worked themselves up for the attack. Johnny Johnson loosed the last three rounds in the rifle magazine into two of the closer hogs and then left the sobbing Simpson on his own to make a run for the boat. The weight of his body slamming into the aluminum john boat drove it off of the gravel shore and beyond the reach of the popping jaws that were so close behind him. For the rest of his life the cowardly rich boy, Jimmy Johnson, would hear the screams of Deputy Simpson as the hogs devoured him alive before turning their attention on the dead of their own kind.

Bob and Tom were still sitting up revisiting the day's activities when the clock on Tessie's mantle dinged ten times.

"What do you say we take a look at our cameras, Bob?" Tom asked, "Maybe something interesting will turn up."

Tom retrieved the latest videos from the online storage and the two men watched in amazement as the john boat of Deputy Simpson was grounded hard on the landing, and a young man came running past the camera.

"Bob, that was the Johnson boy, I'm sure of it!" Tom exclaimed.

"I wonder what in the world he was doing out there, and why would he have the deputy's boat?" Bob replied.

"I haven't got a clue at this point, Bob, but I'll bet my socks that our friendly Sheriff has something to do with it," Tom told him.

They looked at the other camera footage and saw the herd of hogs march past and out of sight in the direction of the landing.

"Want to bet that those had something to do with him coming out in that big hurry?" Bob asked.

"If so, it doesn't bode well for the deputy, he didn't come back," Tom said somberly.

"We need to get these pictures to the Kentucky Wildlife folks. They need to know what they are up against," Bob said.

"They probably haven't been notified about any of this either," Tom replied, "I'll download the files in the morning while you see if anybody remembers your exploits in South Carolina."

"Sounds like a plan to me, Tom, life was starting to get a little boring. I just wish my old partner could have been here to see this. It would have been right up his alley!" Bob told him.

They spent the next two hours telling each other hunting stories, and Bob retold the story of the big cat for the first time since he had buried his partner two years before.

## CHAPTER 10

The old two-story frame home that Tessie Applewhite so generously opened to her guests was built long before the advent of central air conditioning and only had two small window units to cool the two rooms that Tessie used most. Neither of which was the upstairs corner bedroom that Tom and Angie slept in. Tom had opened the corner windows to get a little breeze in the hot room, but the outside heat on this summer evening was still above eighty degrees, making sleep difficult as the sheets under him filled with sweat. He quietly moved an overstuffed chair close to the open window and dozed fitfully, all the while amazed at his wife who could sleep through a hurricane, or, in this instance, a volcano.

"Tommy, Tommy," a voice called out to him.

Tom opened his eyes slightly to see Jeremiah standing in front of him.

"Jeremiah, what in the world…how did you get in here?" Tom stammered.

"Tommy, you are in danger here," the figure in front of him said.

"What are you talking about, Jeremiah? What is the danger?" Tom asked, hoping that Angie would wake up.

"Evil has a grip here, and you have awakened it," he said.

"What evil are you talking about, Jeremiah? I know about the hogs and the demons. We cast one out of John Sprague before somebody killed him this afternoon," Tom told him.

"John Sprague wasn't the only one, Tommy, the others know who you are now," the tone was ominous.

"Well, if we are in danger, what can I do? The sheriff is not going to let us go out of town now," Tom said.

"Strengthen your faith, Tommy, and stay close to Bob Pike, there is safety in numbers," Jeremiah said, "I'll be watching."

With that, Jeremiah turned toward the window and disappeared in a brilliant flash of white light.

"Tom, Tom, wake up. You're having a bad dream!" Tom woke to Angie calling him from the bed.

"Angie, did you see Jeremiah?" Tom asked, his heart still racing from the encounter.

"There was nobody in here but you and me, Tom. What did you see in your dream?" Angie replied.

"Jeremiah was standing right here telling me that we were in danger and that something evil was coming for us, at least that is what I think he said. He also said for us to stick together, that there was safety in numbers," Tom told her.

"You'd better go wake Bob and Abigail up, I believe that whatever this 'Jeremiah' is, he is trying to keep us safe, so let's listen to him," Angie told him.

Before Tom could respond there was a knock at the bedroom door, "Tom, Angie, are you folks awake?" Bob called in a whisper.

"Come on in Bob, we're up," Angie answered.

Bob and Abigail came into the room visibly shaken.

"What's going on, Bob?" Tom asked.

"I just had a vision of sorts that was warning us of danger. It was so real that I thought I was awake!" Bob replied.

"Did the vision have a name?" Angie asked.

"Jeremiah was the name that he gave to me, but that could have been from Tom telling me about his dream the other night," Bob told them.

"Bob was thrashing around in his sleep and calling out that name when I woke him up," Abigail said quietly, "What does it mean?"

"I think that Tom has had a guardian angel since he was a little boy and this angel is trying to keep us safe," Angie told her, "That is basically identical to the dream that Tom had a few minutes ago."

"Well, given what we know is happening in the spiritual realm around here, I think we would be foolish to discount this as a mere dream. The problem is, I just don't know how we are going to prepare for whatever it is that Jeremiah is warning us about," Tom told them, "all he said was that something evil knew who we were."

"What was that you said about strengthening your faith, Tom? Jeremiah told you to strengthen your faith, didn't he?" Angie asked.

"Yes he did, but I wonder what that means exactly?" he replied.

"I think it means that we need to get in the bible and be in prayer until morning, Tom," Bob spoke, "Whatever is coming will find us wherever we are or Jeremiah would have told us to make a run for it. Let's just pray about this and be ready for daybreak."

Daniel Ellis' phone rang at ten pm just as he and Susy were getting ready for bed. The identity was Deputy Simpson.

"Hello Johnny, is everything going smoothly at the dig?" Daniel answered.

"Sheriff Ellis, this is Jimmy Johnson, hogs killed Johnny, and I'm in his truck trying to get somewhere safe," came the hysterical reply.

"Jimmy, you can't be seen anywhere around here. What happened to Johnny, that is Deputy Simpson, and take it real slow so I can understand," Daniel ordered.

"We were at the cave and Johnny was unloading the supplies that you sent when some big hogs attacked us. I killed two of them, but they chased us to the boat. Johnny didn't make it. Oh God, I can still hear his screams," the boy sobbed.

"You left him? How could you do that? Never mind, tell me where you are, and I'll have Deputy Riva pick you up," Daniel waited for the boy to answer but heard only the phone going dead, "Damn!"

"What is it, Danny?" Susy asked.

"Nothing Dear, I have to go out for about an hour, do you want me to pick you up anything while I'm out?" he answered.

"No, just come home quickly," Susy Ellis said with a smile, "and be careful, Sheriff."

Daniel gave her a big hug and headed for the door. Things were getting difficult, and he needed to regain control of the operation before Senator Trent caught wind of his problems. He radioed George Riva to meet him at the landing. Everything hinged on cleaning up any sign of their involvement with the Johnson kid.

"George, Sheriff Ellis here, bring your pickup to the landing, I'll meet you in thirty minutes."

"Sheriff, it's a little late in the evening isn't it?" George replied.

"Yeah, but Johnny has had a little problem and needs our help with the boat." Daniel lied.

"Ten-four, I'm on the way," George came back.

"Oh, and George, make sure that your rifle is loaded," Daniel cautioned.

"Will do, out."

The drive into the unlit Cannon Lake Road was eerie on the best of days, much less coming in at night with just a three-quarter moon to make every shadow look menacing. Daniel slowly drove down to the landing where the john boat belonging to Deputy Simpson was sitting. He played the spotlight of the patrol car across the road and into the woods looking for any sign of the hogs that Johnny had reported but found nothing except shrubbery in its beam.

He pulled the vehicle to the left about fifty yards up the road from the boat so that the headlights would illuminate a broader area, and dreaded having to get out of the SUV to help load the boat. Finally, Deputy Riva's truck came in behind him and turned so that he could back down the ramp. Daniel got out and retrieved his rifle from the trunk, checking to make certain to insert a fresh thirty round magazine and to cycle the bolt to load a round in the chamber.

"Where's Simpson, Daniel?" Riva called as he got out of the truck and lowered the tailgate.

"Dead, as far as I know. That Johnson kid spooked when they were attacked by hogs at the cave, and left him to be eaten," Daniel replied.

Deputy Riva, a hard man that had a soulless look in his dark eyes, seemed unfazed by the news.

"What about the boy?" he asked calmly.

"I don't know where he went, but he called me about ten and told me what had happened. We need to find him and keep him quiet or we'll both end up in the pen," Daniel replied.

Is he in Johnny's truck? If so, we can just run the GPS locator and find out where he is, let's get the boat loaded," Riva said.

"The sooner, the better, I don't want to end up like Evan did," he replied.

They quickly slid the boat into the truck bed and tied it off.

"We'll put it back on the trailer when we find it, and park it at the office. As far as anyone knows, it never was out here," Daniel told him, "I'll make a call for the GPS location now."

Riva led the way out with the truck and Daniel called for a location on the GMC that Simpson drove. Within five minutes, an operator gave them the street number where it could be found. The kid had driven it to Gerald Johnson's car dealership!

Daniel was starting to get the feeling that he was living a nightmare that he couldn't wake up from as he called Riva with the news. How this could get any worse, he wasn't certain, but if past history was an indicator, it was going to.

Daniel pulled up in the car lot and saw the truck with the trailer still attached sitting in front of the trailer that served as the sales office for Gerald Johnson's lot. There were no lights on inside, which meant the kid had probably not contacted anyone yet, and since Daniel had not received any phone calls from either Ruth Ann or Gerald regarding Jimmy, they might not know anything about their son's part in the silver heist that was underway. Right now it seemed like the only option was to call Gerald Johnson and tell him that someone had stolen a truck and parked it on his lot, most likely stealing another car from there as a getaway vehicle.

"Gerald, this is Sheriff Ellis. I hate to bother you this late, but I have a stolen truck sitting in your car lot. Can you come down?" Daniel held his breath.

"Certainly, Sheriff, give me a few minutes, and I'll be right there," was his reply.

Riva pulled up in his patrol car as Daniel was getting out, "Any sign of him?"

"No, I think that the boy must have 'borrowed' a car from the old man so he could hightail it out of here. Gerald is on the way down, so we'll know in a minute what we are looking for," Daniel answered, "I don't want a paper trail on this either, George. We'll just take the truck back to the office and load the boat back on the trailer. Johnny isn't married, so we can put off any report on his disappearance for a couple of days. After we get that silver out, we'll be gone and somebody else can figure this out."

"What about the boy?" Riva asked.

"His parents are already grieving, so just throw the body out in the woods close to the hogs," Daniel answered coldly.

"A man after my own heart," Riva answered with a cold laugh just as Gerald Johnson pulled into the lot in his new Jaguar XJ sedan.

"Hello Sheriff…deputy," he greeted them, "Is that the truck?"

"Yes, but I need to know if any of your inventory is missing, Gerald. Can you do a quick check for us?" Daniel asked politely.

"I'd be happy to, come on in and I'll look at the list. Did you check to see if the front door was open?" he asked.

"No, we wanted to get you out here first, just in case," Daniel covered his rear.

"Well it doesn't seem to be broken into, my key works," Johnson told him as he entered and turn the lights on.

Ten minutes later he gave his assessment, "It looks like everything is here, Sheriff. All of the keys on the keyboard are still there, and I have the car list of what is supposed to be on the lot. As you can see, they are all still there."

If Daniel was puzzled by the news, he didn't show it, "That's good news for you, Gerald; I'm going to take the truck back with me and leave my SUV. Don't sell it while I'm gone."

Gerald Johnson laughed at the bad joke and walked back to the Jag after locking up.

"Let me know if there is anything else that I can do, Sheriff," he said before driving off.

Daniel just waved and then turned angrily to Riva, "We have to find that kid and kill him tonight. Follow me back to the office so I can drop the truck. You can bring me back out here, and we'll start a search."

As they pulled away from the car lot, the one thing that everyone missed was that Jimmy's 1956 Chevy step side was not parked behind the repair shop anymore.

## CHAPTER 11

The house phone ringing downstairs interrupted the prayer meeting being held in Tom and Angie's bedroom. The time was just a little after two am and everyone's nerves were wound up like rubber bands.

"Are you folks awake?" Tessie Applewhite called up the stairwell.

"Yes Ma'am, Miss Applewhite, we're up," Tom answered.

"Well, get on down here, something is going on that you need to know about!" she exclaimed.

Tom hurried to the stairs in his pajamas followed closely by Angie and then the Pikes. Tessie was in the living room with the phone in her hand.

"What's going on Tessie?" Angie asked.

My niece, Doris Hobbs over in Clear Creek is on the phone, and she says that the Johnson boy that got killed is over at her house," Tessie explained, "She is afraid of the sheriff and wants to know what to do with him."

"I'll talk to her," Tom reached for the phone, "Missus Hobbs, this is Tom Strongbow. We're friends of Tessie and might be able to help that boy."

"Mister Strongbow, he just showed up here about an hour ago and I really just want to shoot him for what he put my Emily through, but he is talking crazy things about killer hogs, crooked cops, and silver coins. What am I going to do with him? I can't turn him in to Sheriff Ellis if what he is telling me is true," she told him.

"Give me fifteen minutes, ma'am, and I'll call you back with an answer. Don't do anything until I call, understood?" Tom replied.

"Yes, yes, I'll wait, but please hurry," Doris sounded out of breath.

"Okay folks, here's the situation. Jimmy Johnson is over in Clear Creek with Tessie's great grand niece and her mother. He has the answer to whatever is going on out there on the lake, but is deathly afraid to talk to Daniel or his deputies about it. Now, this thing has gone beyond just demonic hogs killing folks. There is something the boy is telling about a silver cache out there and the sheriff is in on it. If any of this is true, he will be dead by morning unless we come up with a plan to hide him somewhere. Any ideas?" Tom finished.

"We could call the state troopers in and turn this over to them," Bob suggested.

"Well, Daniel has constitutional authority here in this county so he could overrule the state boys. Besides, it would be our word against his, and they would almost certainly side with him,"

"Why can't we just hide him ourselves?" Abigail suggested.

"I think that anybody driving out of here at this hour is going to look suspicious, and I really can't think of a good place to stash the kid away…wait a minute…Josiah Perkins!" Tom lit up like a light bulb; Pastor Perkins would be the logical person to call for help. Nobody would think to look for the boy in Knoxville.

The call to Josiah Perkins found the old man strangely awake as if he had been waiting for it.

"Hello Tom," he answered.

"How did you…never mind sir, we have a problem that you might be able to help us with," Tom explained the situation.

"Of course, I can help, especially if the young man hasn't been charged with anything. We wouldn't want an interstate flight offense piled on him, now would we?" Perkins answered.

Tom gave the old man the address and phone number of Doris Hobbs and then hung up to make the call to Doris. It would take about an hour, maybe two, but Josiah Perkins would get Jimmy out of town until it was safe to bring him back.

"Missus Hobbs, Tom Strongbow here, I've got a pastor from Knoxville coming to pick Jimmy up and take him to a sanctuary down there. Can you hide him until then?" Tom asked.

"Why yes, but his truck is pulled around back of the house. If Sheriff Ellis sees it, he'll know that Jimmy has been here." She sounded worried.

"Do you have a garage, ma'am?" Tom asked.

"Why yes, yes we do. Now why didn't I think of that?" she replied.

Tom heard her shout for Emily to get the truck in the garage and put the car in the driveway out front.

"Pastor Perkins will call when he gets there Missus Hobbs. We just need to sit tight and wait for about an hour or so," Tom said.

"I'll keep him hidden until then Mr. Strongbow. I don't like the boy after what he did to Emily, but I like the politics of that sheriff even less. Besides, his mother has enough grief over losing him once. I'm not about to add to it," Doris replied before hanging up.

"Well, Tom, if the sheriff is chasing around after the boy, he won't be likely to be at the lake. We need to go get your cameras out of there," Bob said.

"He might have someone watching the road at the church. They wouldn't need a light to recognize my truck," Tom replied.

"We'll take our rental car and the heavy rifles. If we have any luck at all, those hogs are somewhere else tonight, and if we don't, we wax a couple of hogs and run," Bob laughed, "besides, the wildlife folks will probably be in there tomorrow and it could get pretty crowded."

"You called them, didn't you?" Tom asked.

"Once a game warden…you know," Bob laughed.

"Angie, we'll be back in about an hour, maybe less. I've got my phone so if anything happens, call me," Tom hugged his wife.

"You men be careful, and I mean it!" Abigail told Bob.

"Yes dear, aren't we always?" Bob smiled.

"I mean it Robert Pike! You aren't a spring chicken anymore." Abigail tried to act cross but the smile gave her away.

The trip to the lake took about thirty minutes, and Bob turned the vehicle lights off once they were close to the George Tuttle Road fork. They idled slowly in to the clearing that Bob would have to cross to get the first camera. Tom picked up the Rigby double from the back seat while Bob got the Remington 30S and loaded three rounds in the magazine and one in the chamber of the 300grain Barnes solids.

Tom decided to walk with Bob in to the area where the camera was and guard his back while it was retrieved.

"I see you've got you Kevlar leggings on, Tom. Don't you think that is kind of unfair that you would have both legs protected and I would have no protection?" Bob observed in a whisper.

"I can let you have the left legging, and I'll take the right leg. That way if we get attacked we'll have two good legs between us," Tom laughed.

"Very funny! Let's get this over with," Bob told him.

They eased quietly to the small tree that held the camera and listened for any sound of the hogs but the woods were quiet.

Tom had the Rigby at the ready with his back to the road in case something came at them from the forest and wasn't paying attention to his back. All of a sudden, there was a cracking of a stick just a few yards behind them and both men spun to meet their attackers. Instead of a herd of vicious hogs, they were looking at a doe and her fawn out for an early morning feeding. They breathed a sigh of relief and Bob turned to finish retrieving the camera when the first of several large hogs charged the two startled men. Tom swung the Rigby quickly and got a point-blank shot off on the first hog that hit the muzzle of the rifle and knocked him over backward.

Bob had grabbed to Remington but had to use it as a club to deflect the tusks of another hog that was intent on ripping his legs out from under him. He quickly recovered and fired a 300-grain bullet into the hog's back as it barreled past him, dropping it instantly. As fast as he could work the bolt, Bob had another round in the rifle and had swung to cover the next charge, but the hogs had retreated into the edge of the woods. Only the sound of their cutters being sharpened gave away their position.

"You all right Tom?" Bob asked without taking his eyes off of the hogs.

"Just my pride is damaged, Bob, although I did kill that first one, so there are two less out here," he replied as he got up, "Let's get the camera and get out of here. Somebody will be along to check on those cannon shots pretty quick, I'll bet."

"What about the other one?" Bob asked.

"We are out of time, let's go," he answered as they backed to the car without taking their eyes or their flashlights off of the wood line.

As they reached the end of Cannon Creek Lake road, they saw the sky lit up with flashing lights and headed their way. Bob pulled the car in behind the church building and shut the lights off, using the emergency brake to stop it. Seconds later, two sheriff's department vehicles roared past the church on the narrow road within feet of their car, but they were unseen.

"Now would be a good time to get this thing out of here, Bob. Can you run with the lights off?" Tom asked.

"Piece of cake, Tom. I got my training sneaking up on poachers, and now I am one!" he laughed.

They made the run back to Tessie's without any problems, which surprised Tom who envisioned a speeding ticket from one of the town policemen who were ever vigilant when it came to filling the city coffers with fines money. They rushed upstairs and into their pajamas, hiding the rifles in Tessie's bedroom when they came in. In less than thirty minutes a car slid to a stop outside the house and someone started knocking at the door.

Tessie, acting like she had been sound asleep answered the door, "Yes, who is it?"

"Miss Applewhite, It's Deputy George Riva, sheriff's department. Can I come in?" he asked.

"My guests are asleep deputy, won't this wait until morning?" she answered sweetly.

"No Ma'am, I have an order from Sheriff Ellis to check inside. I can get a warrant if necessary," he responded.

"That won't be necessary deputy," Tessie slid back the bolt and opened the door, "If you would be so kind to wait in the living room, I'll inform Mr. Strongbow that you are here."

Tom opened the door to the bedroom and asked in a sleepy voice, "Miss Tessie, is everything all right?"

"There is a deputy Riva here to see you, Tommy," she called out and went back to her room.

Tom came down the stairs and into the living room, "What's this about, Riva?"

"Have you and the game warden been home all night?" came the curt response.

"Of course, we have, deputy. There aren't too many places to go in Pineville late at night," Tom answered.

"You weren't at the lake then?" he questioned.

"I didn't lose anything out there so there would be no reason for me to go back out there in the daytime, much less after dark. Why, what is going on?" Tom feigned interest.

"Nothing, Sheriff Ellis wants to make sure you stay put is all," Riva lied.

"I'm going back to bed unless you want anything else. Tell Daniel that we are staying put," Tom turned and walked off in a bluff.

Riva walked to the door before turning back, "I'm watching you Strongbow so don't get any ideas."

Tom couldn't resist the urge, "Or what, you'll take care of me the way you did John Sprague? You might find that I am a little bit harder to kill than that man."

Riva just gave him a deadly stare before stomping out and slamming the door.

"Tommy, I'm so proud of you," Miss Tessie called out, "I wanted to tell him off myself, but I'm too much of a lady."

"Yes Miss Tessie, now go back to bed, we've got an early morning." He replied while stifling a laugh.

## CHAPTER 12

A loud crash of thunder blasted Tom awake at six-thirty, just a couple of hours after they had finally gotten to sleep. Outside a summer storm was bringing heavy rain and lightning to the area, but it was also going to hamper any efforts to track the hogs and bring an end to their murderous rampage.

Angie came into the bedroom, "Come on, Tom, we've fixed breakfast for you late nighters. Today is a big day."

"I'm awake after that explosion outside. How hard is it raining?" he asked groggily.

"It's been heavy, but the forecast is for this to pass over about noon. Come on, Bob and Abigail are waiting for us," Angie replied.

"On the way," he replied as he swung his legs out of the bed, "Did Tessie hear from her niece this morning?"

Angie's voice came back from the hallway, "Yes, everything is fine there now."

"Hey there, outlaw!" Bob greeted him in the dining room, "I told Tessie that you'd be taking your eggs 'poached' this morning."

Tom laughed at the reference to their clandestine activities of the night before.

"So what is the game plan with the wildlife folks, Bob?" he asked

"I'm supposed to get a call when they get to the lake. The weather might slow that down a bit, though," Bob answered.

"I've been giving this some thought, Bob. Could those demons come out of the pigs at will? I'm a little unclear about that." Tom asked.

"I suppose that they could, although my guess is that they are looking for a suitable human host. They couldn't attack us when we killed those last night because, as Christians, we have the Holy Spirit indwelling. The scripture says that light and darkness cannot exist in the same place, so we are safe from being possessed. Not that a demon can't really mess up your day from the outside!" Bob tried to answer.

"I heard you send the one from John Sprague to the Abyss, but what about those that were in the hogs last night? Where did they go?" Tom asked.

"I really don't know, but possibly they are looking for something else to hitch a ride in," he answered, "which is why it is important that we knock the animal down, cast the demons into the pit, and then dispatch the hog. At least I think that's what Josiah was trying to tell us to do."

"Okay men, enough shop talk, it's time for some of Tessie's famous biscuits and gravy," Tessie announced as she carried in a plate of fresh biscuits followed by Angie and Abigail with the gravy and a bowl of fresh sugared strawberries.

"Miss Tessie, this is my favorite, how did you know?" Tom asked.

Well, Angie told me this morning, and Abigail told me that Bob was awfully fond of strawberries on his biscuits with whipped cream. I sugared those last night so they would have plenty of juice. Now eat up, there's plenty," Tessie beamed.

"Tom," Bob spoke after they had eaten, "how well do you know the area around the lake?"

"Well, it's been years since I was in those hills, but I can probably find my way in and out all right, why?" he answered.

"I'm thinking that we should go up that road that bears to the left and then see if we can get around the lake to find where they went with the john boat last night. As wet as it is, I don't think the sheriff will be up there this morning, so he won't see your truck if we hide it in the woods once we get in," Bob told him.

"I don't know what we are looking for, but it couldn't hurt to go check that area out before the wildlife folks get there. Besides, they will keep Daniel Ellis distracted and off of us anyway." Tom said, "Sounds like a plan. Let's get cleaned up and get out there."

They made the run in a heavy rain to the lake access road and then onto George Tuttle road without seeing another person, although the road was home to several trailers and double-wides, some abandoned. Tom found a spot that would give them a short hike to the end of the lake, and they backed the truck up into the woods and out of sight of the casual observer.

"That's going to be quite a little hike, Tom. Where are we going to look first after we get around the end there?" Bob asked.

"Well, I'm thinking that they must have dragged the john boat up on the shore if they were going to load anything in it, so let's get around there and start walking the shoreline in those coves," he replied, shouldering the Rigby that was wrapped in a rainproof poncho.

Bob was carrying the Remington again and had likewise covered it with a piece of plastic that they cut off of a blue tarp that Tom carried in the vehicle. They hiked across the rough terrain around the end of the lake aided by four wheeler trails that seemed to run everywhere through the backcountry and finally reached what they thought would be a good place to start looking after walking almost two miles.

The cove that looked like a finger jutting into the hills was actually a valley that was filled with water when the dam had been built. Except for the head of the cove where it seemed to be flat, the sides were steep and wouldn't have provided any access to a boat. They made their way slowly and carefully around the cove until they reached the sand and gravel area at the end. The rain had obliterated any tracks or skid marks the boat had made, but they searched thoroughly anyway.

"Bob, over here, there appears to be a path leading up this hill a little ways," Tom called in a low voice.

Bob came over and looked at what might have been a game trail only this was wider. Since it had stopped raining, he took the blue tarp off of the rifle and chambered a 300 grain round.

"Let's have a look," Bob said as he took point.

Tom also cleared the big Rigby for action, making sure that there were two 400 grain bullets in the chambers.

They hadn't gone very far when something in the brush to their left attracted their attention. Badly mangled, but unmistakable in appearance was the head of Johnny Simpson. Both men looked the other way quickly at the sight.

"We need to get somebody's attention, Bob," Tom said while trying to keep breakfast down.

"That's never easy to see, Tom, but he's not going anywhere for a while, let's keep looking," Bob replied.

They eased along the path for another thirty yards when the opening of the cave became visible in front of them in a rock outcropping. Just outside was the evidence of a campfire with the cooking irons still set up and a stack of plastic storage tubs that had been tipped over. Someone had abandoned this place quickly and for what was now an obvious reason. In the short brush, a few yards away appeared to be a partially eaten hog. They exchanged looks momentarily and then with a nod from Bob, started through the narrow opening in single file. Bob took his LED light from a pocket and illuminated the dark cavern that the small opening brought them into. It appeared to be about twenty feet across and much deeper with a ceiling of about ten feet. There was also evidence that someone had been staying here recently judging by the bedroll and backpack that was on the floor of the cave and the Coleman lantern that was sitting on a rock.

After lighting the lantern, they moved back into the recess of the cave another few yards before a pile of rotting wooden boxes partially covered by rocks caught their eye. On closer examination, both men were rendered speechless by the discovery. In the pile before them were thousands of silver cobs, money struck from a silver bar in the style of the Spanish in the late sixteen hundreds and early seventeen hundreds.

"Bob, this must be the lost Swift silver that people have been looking for since Swift left it here almost three hundred years ago. Holy cow, I remember my dad talking about how he and his friends looked all over Pine Mountain for this cave, and here it is way over here," Tom told him.

"I've never seen anything like this, Tom. How much do you think it's worth?" he asked.

I have no idea, Bob, but I'll bet it is worth enough for some folks to kill for," Tom replied, "Put a couple of those in your pocket, and let's ease out of here."

"What are we going to do with the deputy out there?" Bob asked.

Tom thought for a minute, "It seems obvious that we can't tell anyone about where the head is now because we might disappear, but we could move it back over to the landing and let somebody else find it, say the wildlife folks."

"That seems pretty gruesome, but he is already wherever he is going to be for eternity, I'm sure Johnny won't mind if we move the head. Besides, I have an idea where the rest of him might be, and that is even worse," Bob replied with a grimace.

Tom retrieved the pack after they put some silver coins in their pockets, and they made their way carefully back to pick up Johnny Simpson's head. Bob used the piece of blue tarp to wrap it in before the gently slid it into the pack.

"Let's get this out of here, Tom," he said as a shiver went through him, "I don't feel like finding those hogs in this cover."

After Tom marked the location of the cave mouth with his Garmin, they made a straight line hike back to the truck and checked the surroundings before stepping out into the open. With nobody in sight, Tom put the pack containing the head in the back and they eased out on the road for the most nerve-wracking part of the trip, placing the head where the camera had been the night before. Fortunately, they had no visitors since the continuing thunder claps were keeping any boaters off of the lake. Being careful to keep their tracks hidden, they quickly placed the deputy's mortal remains in the clearing and made a double-time run for the truck. Both men felt a huge sense of relief when they were back on 25E headed north. Now it was up to the wildlife folks to get there, and Daniel Ellis would not have a notion that his treasure trove had been found.

## CHAPTER 13

"Ellis, this has been dragging on long enough. Now I want the location of that mine revealed so I can get some men in there to do what you and this hired ape don't seem to be able to do," Senator Trent said sharply.

"That is not going to happen, Senator. Jimmy Johnson, Deputy Simpson, and I are the only ones that know where the cave is located, and Simpson is missing along with the boy," Daniel told him.

"What? We have ten million dollars in cash waiting for that silver to board a private jet in Knoxville! TEN MILLION DOLLARS! Isn't that enough incentive for you to get your little band of merry men together and bring that silver out?" Trent was furious.

"Believe me, I wish that this was over, but between those hogs and Tom Strongbow, I'm at my wits end," he replied.

"Strongbow? I knew his family. Why don't you let me deal with Mr. Strongbow? Sometimes we can gather more flies with sugar than your methods," Trent suggested strongly.

George Riva visibly strained to repress the urge to strike the old man that sat across the polished mahogany desk, but he knew that the bodyguard that was ever present would make mincemeat out of him in seconds.

"I will arrange a meeting with Tom, sir, although I don't see how you can convince him that not causing us trouble over Sprague's death is in his best interest," Daniel answered.

"I have methods a mountain low brow like you will never understand Ellis, just get him in here to see me as quickly as possible," Trent ordered.

Daniel exited without another word and took Riva with him, "This is all falling apart because you killed John Sprague, George. If you had only curbed that temper just this one time, we would be rich men."

Riva just gave him a dark look but kept silent.


Tom's cell phone rang shortly after two pm, "Tommy, Daniel Ellis here. Listen, we really got off on the wrong foot and I want to make it up to you. An old friend of your family wants to talk to you and get this smoothed over. Can we set up a meeting?"

"Who's the 'old friend' Daniel?" Tom asked.

"Senator Andrew Trent, Tommy. He knows your family," Daniel told him.

Tom thought briefly and then replied, "Sure, why not. Go ahead and set the meeting up and call me back,"

"No need, Tommy. He's waiting for us in his office. How about thirty minutes?" Ellis asked.

Bob was standing in front of Tom shaking his head in the negative, but Tom decided to go along.

"Okay, I'll meet you in thirty minutes. I know where the Senator keeps his office," Tom told him and ended the call.

"Tom, have you gone nuts?" Bob asked, "These people are going to kill us if we cozy up to them. There is too much money involved, and how about the dead guy?"

"I'll be fine, Bob. They don't know that we have the videos, and they don't know that we found the cave. You work with the wildlife people and make sure that they find that head. If you can, take our wives to Tazewell and see if that roadside motel of the same name has a room in the back. The place is clean and certainly far enough away that nobody can find them. I should be finished with the Senator by the time that you get back," Daniel said.

They pulled up at Tessie's as Angie and Abigail were getting into the Pike's rental.

"Where are you all going?" Tom asked.

"We've been invited to a little afternoon tea with Miss Tessie. It will be a break from all of the strange things that have been going on," Angie told him.

"Do you think that is a good idea? The sheriff just called and wants me to meet with a very heavy hitter named Senator Trent. It can't be good news," Tom told her, deciding to keep the silver find a secret for the time being.

"We'll be fine, Tom. I promise," Angie told him.

"Okay, but stay close to your phone in case we have to leave in a hurry," Tom gave in.

Bob just gave him a funny look and got back in the truck, "I'm stuck with you then, partner. They've got my car."

"Let's go see what the senator wants," Tom said and backed out of the drive.

They were met at the door of Andrew Trent's expansive office by a no-nonsense looking figure of a man that had 'hired mercenary' written all over his look, especially since he made no effort to conceal the Glock 21 in the waistband holster.

After a brief pat down, they were ushered into the office where Senator Trent was coming around the desk to meet them, his best campaign smile adorning his face.

"Welcome, Tom, and I assume this is your friend Bob Pike, the retired game warden?" he asked.

"Good afternoon senator, yes this is Bob Pike, retired from the South Carolina Department of Wildlife, now currently pastoring a church in Honduras," he replied.

"Welcome, Bob, come on in and have a seat," he waved his hand to the red leather chairs facing a couch of the same.

"Tom, I was talking to Sheriff Ellis today about the unfortunate death of John Sprague during a routine questioning, and he told me that somehow, they had made a mistaken judgment call that the death involved you and Bob. As a ranking board member of this community, I want to clear the air about this, and apologize for the sheriff who feels that your animosity towards him might keep you from accepting his apology," Trent said.

Tom looked briefly at Bob and then replied, "I would be happy to accept Daniel's apology, Sir. We wanted to get back to our families by the day after tomorrow, and I was afraid that Daniel's order for us not to stray from town might affect that timetable."

"Consider it a misunderstanding, Tom. You know, your grandfather and I had an interesting relationship way back in the day. I remember when your family would come to visit him, and I believe that we met a time or two at his office. It's been good seeing you again, and please give my regards to your lovely wife. I believe that she and Mrs. Pike are having tea with my wife and Tessie Applewhite this afternoon," he concluded, standing to dismiss them.

A cold chill ran up Tom's spine as he realized that he and Bob had just been delivered a subtle threat that involved the safety of their wives if they caused any more trouble for Daniel and the senator.

"Thanks for clearing everything up, Sir. You can assure Daniel that we'll be no more trouble," Tom led Bob out of the office.

Neither man spoke until they were safely in the heavy Ford, and then Bob said, "What in the Hell was that all about?"

"That, my friend was a very high placed and corrupt ex-politician telling us that unless we complied, we are going to be in deep trouble," Tom told him, "See if you can get Abigail on the phone. We need to relocate immediately!"

While Bob was contacting his wife, Tom had Siri call the number for the Tazewell Motor Lodge. The manager answered on the first ring.

"Have you got two rooms on the back side of the motel for a couple of nights?" Tom asked, "Great, book me for two adjoining rooms, and I need to make certain that they are in the back of the building away from the highway. My wife has trouble sleeping with road noise. Yes, we'll be in tonight."

After making the reservations, Tom turned to Bob, "We will be safe down there in Tazewell. That motel is small and private, but very clean."

"Abigail says that they will be back at Tessie's in about a half an hour and that we should go ahead and pack," Bob replied.

"I need to get Milton's rifles back to him also. Maybe I can do that before they get back so we can leave ASAP," Tom said.

Tom cleaned the rifles with a kit that he kept in the truck and made the run back to Milton Bunch's house while Bob got things ready at Tessie's. Milton met him at the door.

"Hello Tom, did you men have any luck?" he asked.

"Yes, sir, but we didn't get the one that we were after. We also stirred up a hornets' nest with Senator Trent and Daniel Ellis so I thought we'd get these back before we left," Tom told him.

"Senator Trent, eh?" Milton looked interested, "what is that pirate up to with the sheriff, I wonder?"

Tom decided that this was a man that could be trusted so he stuck his hand in his trouser pocket and pulled out one of the silver eight reale pieces.

"Whew," the old man whistled, "I've seen pictures of these but never held one in my hand. Where did you find it, Tom?"

Tom was evasive about the location, "Well, I think that this may be the lost Swift silver that folks have spent the last three-hundred years looking for."

"It could be, it could be at that. The Swift silver was a bootleg operation where he was casting bars from a mine near about, and then cutting off an eight reale slice before marking it with a heavy hammer blow to imprint the shield and Jerusalem Cross. Notice how the edges are split and the embossing is uneven? That is the way most Spanish currencies looked before we started making mill pieces late in the seventeen hundreds," Milt informed him.

"What do you think it might be worth?" Tom asked.

"I can't say for sure, but I would hazard a guess that a minimum amount would be one hundred dollars and maybe as high as one thousand dollars. How many are there?" he asked.

"Well, I didn't count them, but I would say more than one hundred thousand!" Tom told him.

"Legend has it that Swift left two hundred and fifty thousand in the great Shawnee cave on his last trip, but nobody has ever found it. I even looked for it myself when I was younger. I sure wish that

I had one in my collection, what a trophy that would be," the old man mused.

"Milton, why don't you keep that one? I picked up two, and you've been a big help to us with the rifles," Tom told him, "Just keep quiet about having it. I think there is a lot of danger involved if anyone finds out that I found that cave."

"Tom, I don't use those rifles anymore, and I don't have any children to leave them to. I would be proud for you to keep them to remember me by in exchange for this gift of the silver," Milt shook Tom's hand.

"Why, thank you sir, but those rifles are worth more than that silver," Tom protested.

"Son, an object is worth only as much as the value the owner puts on it. I happen to value the gift of the silver more than the rifles, so take them with my blessings," Milton replied.

Tom picked the rifles back up and headed out the door, "Goodbye Milt, I hope to see you again soon."

"You too Tom, I'll tell Agnes that you folks left town, that way everybody will know as soon as she can pull her phone out," Milton laughed.

Tom loaded the rifles into the back seat and headed the Ford back to Tessie Applewhite's, arriving just as Abigail was pulling into the driveway with Angie and Tessie.

Angie gave him a hug and asked, "What's going on Tom? Abigail said that we would be leaving."

"We have to get you all to a safe place, so Bob and I can finish the job that Josiah gave us. We also can't tell Tessie that we aren't going home either. She will be in danger if she knows where we are," Tom told her quietly, "I'll explain everything once we are on the road."

"Let me go in and pack our toiletries. You get our clothes loaded. We can be out of here in thirty minutes," Angie told him.

Chalk it up to the harrowing experience of running from the FBI, but it didn't slip Bob Pike's glance that they were being watched by a dark gray SUV that was parked down the street about two blocks. It had circled the block twice since Tom had gone to Milt's and was now just parked, but the man behind the wheel looked suspiciously like the bozo that had patted them down earlier. Tom needed to know before they pulled out in tandem to leave. When they got inside, Bob gave him the news out of earshot of their wives and Tessie.

"Well, I've never had to worry about being tailed Bob, what do we do now?" Tom asked.

"I'm going to leave first with Abigail because I don't think that he will follow me. Somewhere down the road, I will get out of sight and wait for him to pass me while following you. Once I get behind him, I'll get his tag number and see if one of my new friends in the wildlife department can get him pulled for a poaching inspection or something. A bunch of these fellows remember us from those cougar days," Bob told him.

"I think that you miss the thrill of the chase, Bob," Tom laughed, "Well it's not much, but it is a better plan than I've got. Oh, Milton gifted us with those rifles."

"You're kidding me, right? That Rigby is worth at least eight grand," Bob replied in shock.

"We'll I traded him a silver cob for them…sort of. You probably should take the Remington with you, just in case," Tom told him.

"Gladly, let's finish up and put this in action. If we shake him, we can get to the room unseen," Bob said as he walked back to the house.

The rest of the packing was without incident, but the gray SUV was still parked up the street until Bob and Abigail pulled out in the rental Chevy. As soon as they cleared the corner, the SUV came down the street and turned after them.

"So much for a plan coming together," Tom told Angie, "We need to go now so we can keep up with Bob."

They said their goodbye to Tessie and left hurriedly to make the turn onto 25E just behind the SUV that had gotten caught at a light. Bob was already out of sight around the long sweeping curve in the highway and Tom guessed that he was exceeding the speed limit slightly. The SUV driver was watching Tom in the rearview mirror and missed the light change. Just as the light turned red, he punched the accelerator and squealed out into the intersection causing several motorists to slam on the brakes and blow their horns. None of which went unnoticed to the Pineville Police Cruiser that was sitting down the street. After the light changed, Tom and Angie drove slowly by the scene of the gray SUV sitting on the side of the highway with two PD cruisers blocking the front and the back, and a Kentucky State Trooper making his way to the man that was spread-eagled on the gray hood.

"I wonder if Jeremiah had anything to do with that, Tom. It certain is a heavenly intervention if I've ever seen one," Angie said.

"Well, I thank the Lord for it, even though we are supposed to pray for our enemies. Let's see if we can get to the motel without any more excitement," he replied.

Bob and Angie were in the office when they arrived, "Tom, the wildlife people are out at the lake. I herded them in the direction of where we wanted them to go, but I think we need to be there in case those hogs show up."

"I think that is going to be risky if the sheriff shows up with his thug, Riva. I'm not sure that I want him to know that we know about the deputy yet," Tom replied.

"Tom, why can't Abigail and I download those videos onto a disk for you while you are gone? They have a good wifi here, and I've got my laptop along. It could certainly give you a bargaining chip if things get rough," Angie told him.

"Okay, great idea, but I think that Bob and I need to go in the rental car. It's not as conspicuous as the truck with my lodge info all over the place," he replied, "Let's get our stuff in the rooms, and then we'll head out."

Both men were full of anxiety during the drive back to the Cannon Creek Lake landing. The big unknown was if the sheriff would show up, certainly a definite possibility, given that his deputy's head was lying in the clearing. Well, if they wanted to have a chance to get the demons out of the hog before they were set loose by the unsuspecting wildlife officers, they would have to chance it.

When they pulled up to the Tuttle road intersection, they could see that there were official vehicles parked on both sides of the road along with an ambulance across from the clearing. The two men got out and walked as casually as possible to the SUV that had the wildlife enforcement emblems and the blue top light.

"Are you Captain Bob Pike?" a young officer asked as they walked up.

"Well, not Captain anymore, just Bob," he answered, "This is a professional hunter friend of mine from South Carolina. Tom Strongbow."

"Pleased to meet you, men. I'm Joe Cloud, the local wildlife officer for this area.

"Cherokee, Joe?" Tom asked.

"Yes I am, as I'm certain that you are with a name like Strongbow," he laughed, "My folks have been around here a very long time, but I've never heard of some of the things that these others have been telling about these hogs."

"Well, we kind of got involved after that boy disappeared when we were pressed into a search party last Sunday. Tom here got hit on the head up there a ways and almost became food for that herd. We also found a school ring in some droppings and saw the fingers of Mr. Meyers when the sheriff called us to the morgue. They had the boy's bracelet that was in one of the hogs Tom killed when he and the sheriff got cornered up there right after Mr. Meyer's death," Bob told him.

"Now I wonder why the sheriff hasn't gotten me involved in this? We've got hogs supposedly killing and eating people and Wildlife doesn't get called. Something doesn't add up," Joe told them.

They were interrupted by one of the men in the upper part of the clearing waving his arms.

"Let's walk up there, they want to see me about something," Joe said and walked away.

Tom and Bob already knew what they had found, but acted unawares until they got to the location where Deputy Simpson's head was lying.

"My God!" Joe exclaimed as they showed the grisly find to him, "Who is that?"

Bob forced himself to take a look at the head again and pause for a few seconds as if trying to figure out who it belonged to, "Unless I miss my guess, that is the head of one of the deputies, Johnny Simpson."

Tom looked quickly at the head and acted as if he was going to throw up, "That's him."

"Get this entire area tied off and get Sheriff Ellis on the phone. We are going to need the state forensics boys down here so somebody start setting up the lights," Joe gave the orders that would secure the area, "How big were the hogs that you killed, Strongbow?"

"Around five hundred apiece. They were well fed, but there is something else that you need to know. One of these hogs is well over a thousand pounds, and he is not just a hog," Tom took a long shot.

Joe Cloud just looked at him for the better part of a minute, "What are you trying to say?"

"Do you remember any of the Cherokee stories about the Kalona Ayelisk that folks told their children to frighten them?" Tom asked.

"Well, I don't hold with much of the old Indian spiritualism being a born again Christian, but I do remember the fallen angel they talked about. I always thought it was a remarkable parallel to Satan rebelling against God and being cast out," he replied, "What has that got to do with this?"

"We've been told that these hogs may have inadvertently received a horde of demons during an exorcism that was performed down George Tuttle Road about five years ago. Now I don't have much knowledge of demonic activity in animals, but my flock in Honduras is regularly fighting against some of the Voodoo practitioners that exhibit classic demon possession. We have been told that this hog needs to be knocked down before the demons are cast into the pit or abyss, and then killed or they will just find another host," Bob answered.

"You guys are crazy!" Joe said in a whisper, "I'll be laughed out of Kentucky if anybody thinks that I'm looking for demon possessed hogs!"

"Then let us take care of them. I've already killed those two, but we haven't found more than a track of the big boar," Tom said, careful not to tell about the other three that they knew to be dead.

"I would be more inclined to believe you if I had a picture of a hog as big as the one that you're talking about. I've never heard of them getting more than about three hundred, maybe four," Joe said.

"These hogs have been feeding on men, Joe. We know that at least three have been eaten, but what about the disappearances of the drug addicts that come out here?" Bob said.

"Let me think on this tonight. I'll give you a call in the morning at first light. We'll have some dogs in here by then. Good meeting both of you," Joe shook their hands and then returned to the gruesome find.

As Bob reached George Tuttle Road they saw the car of Sheriff Daniel Ellis coming up the narrow lake access at a high rate of speed followed by the local news affiliate's van complete with a satellite link. Bob quickly made a right-hand turn, and the cruiser flew behind them without Daniel noticing their presence.

"Well, timing is indeed everything, Tom. Let's go get something to eat, I'm starving," Bob said as he turned the car around.

"Dinner and then a nap if we are getting up at 'Oh dark thirty' tomorrow," Tom replied, "We need to get that hog tomorrow or somebody else can have him as far as I'm concerned. I'm ready to get back to a regular hunt, although we'll never look at an animal the same way after this."

## CHAPTER 14

The monotonous whine of the generator powering the powerful flood lights that Joe Cloud had positioned around the clearing grated on the big hog's nerves causing him to chomp his jaws and tear into the shrubs and brush around him. The other hogs that were left gave him a wide berth because, although they were themselves massive in size, they were no match for the bulk of the twelve hundred pounder or his temperament which was always nasty.

Turel sensed that the time to move his pack of demons out of this animal was close at hand, but they needed to be very careful that the hog wasn't killed before they could make a transition to another host. While the presence of the demonic horde seemed to go unnoticed in the big animal, he had become increasingly psychotic because of all the noise in his head. Tonight the hum of the generator exacerbated the condition and the hog was intent on killing anything remotely connected to the hum. The popping of his jaws increased in frequency as two figures moved closer to the edge of the woods at the bottom of the hill where he and the others waited. Turel was exerting all of his influence now to keep the animal in check but expected the attack to come at any minute.

The timing couldn't be worse for the demon leader either. He sensed that both of the men that the hog was fixating on were Christians, and they needed someone that had not submitted to their enemy if they were going to find another dwelling place. The other problem was the hog's penchant for killing and eating his victims before Turel could act. His only hope now was to unleash the spirit of infirmity against the hog and hope that it would get sick enough to withdraw but not sick enough to die. Turel gave the command to attack and waited nervously for any results that might bear fruit.


"Sheriff Ellis, can you come up here?" Joe called out.

Daniel turned away from his deputy and headed up the hill to where the game warden and another wildlife officer were squatting and looking at the ground.

"What is it?" he asked holding his AR platform rifle loosely.

"We haven't had much luck looking for tracks because of the rain earlier, but we did find one that isn't completely washed out. Is anyone running cows up here?" Joe asked.

Daniel shined his light into the woods, "Officer, I think that I should tell you that there is a very mean bunch of hogs close by and the leader, if I can call him that, is huge, and we are not sufficiently armed Why don't we move back into the relative safety of the vehicles and discuss this?"

To Joe Cloud, the relatively recent arrival of hogs into Kentucky not far from where they were gathered wasn't something to be taken seriously other than the fact that they were nuisance animals that destroyed crops. While he was a very competent wildlife officer, most of Joe's experience was in dealing with elk poachers or teaching hunting safety. Outside of stories from Texas, he had not even heard of a hog eating a man, much less a herd of hogs that regularly foraged on them.

"If you had called us when these animals first killed up here, we wouldn't be out here tonight, and your deputy might still be alive along with Mr. Meyers. Even after Tom Strongbow shot the ones up the hill here and saved your bacon, you didn't call this in. I think that you are going to have a lot to answer for sheriff," Joe told him.

"I'm going to give you a warning, Joe. I am the only constitutional authority present, and you are here at my forbearance. One more threat against me or my judgment, and you will pack this circus up and go home. Is that clear enough for you?" Ellis erupted.

"Perfectly clear, Sheriff. I'll just focus on removing this herd of hogs from the area and let you investigate the deaths," Joe buried his anger.

Daniel Ellis stomped off back to his cruiser, and Joe signaled for his helper to return to the truck. Before leaving the wood line, he shined his light into the forest for about twenty yards. Shining in the light were the eyes of at least a dozen animals including a set that stood much higher and glowed red. His heart seemed frozen in fear for a second as he made a hasty retreat back to the truck without taking his eyes off of the woods. Jerking open the back door on the driver's side, Joe took out his 700 Remington ADL in 30-06 caliber and fumbled to load the magazine with cartridges but was having a time due to his shaking hands.

"Trouble, Joe?" one of the fisheries and wildlife men asked.

"I saw those hogs, Derrick. Tell everyone to move back to the vehicles and arm themselves," he replied.


"We've lost track of Strongbow and Pike, Ellis. Do you have any idea where they might have gone?" Andrew Trent asked Daniel.

"No Sir, and I've got my hands full out here at the lake. Simpson's head was found, and the news van is out here filming.

Someone also called Fish and Game about the hogs. Would you like to hazard a guess who?" Daniel responded angrily.

"Settle down, Ellis. We have lost a little ground with all of the publicity, but it might be a blessing to divert attention away from the silver. If you will just give me the location, I can have people go in there and retrieve it with no one being the wiser," Trent told him.

Knowing that the cave location was the only ace that he held in the game, Daniel kept it very close to his chest. Besides, it was his thought all along that several thousand of those cobs would end up in his coffer as a hedge against future hard times, but that all depended on Trent not knowing where they were now.

"No thanks, Senator. We will have to kill these hogs first, and then I will personally deliver that silver to you. If that buyer won't wait, I'm sure that you can find another one," Daniel answered him.

"You are making a big mistake in underestimating me, Ellis. Get this finished and tie up any loose ends. You have until Saturday," Trent shouted and ended the call.

Daniel was standing by the open door of the patrol car when the call ended. He looked to his left and was surprised to see the game warden crouched behind the front of his truck with a rifle lying on the hood so he walked over.

"Joe, what in the world are you doing?" he asked the obviously frightened man.

"I saw those hogs, Sheriff. One of them is a monster with red eyes!" Joe told him, "Right after you walked away, I played my light into the woods, and there were eyes all over the place about twenty yards away. When I saw the big one looking at me, it was like an ice cube dropped in my soul."

"You've been watching too much late night TV, Joe. These are just hogs that have found out that we taste better than roots, that's all," Daniel said, "regardless of all those stories that are floating around about demons."

"Whatever they are. I'm not going near there again until daybreak, and I darn sure won't go up there without my rifle!" he exclaimed.

"Which is exactly what I suggested now isn't it?" Daniel asked, "Look, it's late and I need some sleep. Let  all of these folks go home and we'll meet back here at daylight."

"I was going to stay here tonight, but no way that is going to happen now. I'll take care of my people of you will handle the reporters," Joe sounded relieved.

"Sounds good, and I'll meet you here at daybreak. By the way, were two fellows from South Carolina here today?" Daniel asked innocently.

"You mean Tom Strongbow and Bob Pike? Yeah they were, but Pike is a retired game warden from South Carolina," he replied.

"I always get them mixed up. Well, goodnight and I'll see you in the morning," Daniel told him as he walked off to handle the news crew.

So the trouble makers hadn't disappeared after all. Tomorrow there might just have to be a couple of hog victims added to the list...if they showed up, and Daniel was certain that they would. He called George Riva.

"George is your cousin Eddie out of the pen yet?" Daniel asked.

"Yeah, last week he called his mother. Why," Riva answered.

"I've got a job for you two in the morning. It will pay really well," Daniel told him, "You will have to be in the woods up here above where Evan Meyers was killed. Your two friends are going to be here to track those hogs. They need to have an accident."

"How much does it pay?" Riva asked.

"Ten thousand for the job, but it has to look like a hunting accident," Daniel told him.

"Consider it done, sheriff. I would almost do that Strongbow character for nothing," he said.

"Riva, be in there before daylight and don't mess this up," Daniel warned before ending the call.

Daniel knew that George Riva had worked as a Mercenary for one of the contractors in Iraq and in Saudi Arabia before striking off on his own down in South America. If anyone could handle this assignment in a cold, calculating manner, George could. Sheriff Ellis made sure that the news crew had left, and then he drove home.

## CHAPTER 15

There was a knock on Andrew Trent's office door before it was opened by the hulking bodyguard, "Excuse me, Senator, but there is a gentleman here to see you. He says it is urgent."

"Who is it, Monroe?" Trent answered.

"He says that he is Milton Bunch and that he an old friend of yours," Monroe replied.

"Yes, yes, show him in," Trent put on his biggest campaign smile as he walked around the desk to greet his old friend and hunting companion, "Hello Milt, it's been much too long. How is Agnes doing?"

"Hello Andy, I'm not here to socialize. There is something going on that you should know about," Milt said.

"Well, what is it, Milt? Is it so serious that we can't catch up on old times?" Trent seemed hurt.

Milt took the silver cob from his pocket and flipped to Trent who caught it and stared in amazement.

"What…where did you get this Milt?" Trent was surprised beyond words.

"Tom Strongbow brought it by the house earlier. It appears that he has found the cave where your stash is," Milt told him.

"Are you certain of this, Milt? Did he say how much he found?" Trent had sweat running down his forehead now.

"He threw out a number higher than one hundred thousand pieces," Milt replied, "I thought that this news was worth the risk in coming over. Folks around here think that I'm a rabid opponent of your Washington schemes, and I would like to keep it that way."

"Well, I think the risk is justified, Milt. After all, you stand to make more on this deal than I do," Trent reminded him.

"Only if you keep your end of the bargain and get that silver to the plane by Saturday at the latest!" Milt replied, "I borrowed up the ten million in good faith based on your promise that Sheriff Ellis and his men could pull this off quietly. How difficult is that going to be to return, do you think?"

"Well, there have been operational expenses, Milt, you understand," Trent told him.

"I might understand and then again, I might not. One thing that I know for sure is that the man who gave me the money on a promise will not understand and neither your elevated position nor your bodyguard will protect you and me from him!" Milt headed for the door, "Saturday, Andrew, no more delays."

After Milt left, Andrew Trent sat at his desk turning the silver reale in his hand slowly. If Tom Strongbow knew about the silver, then his friend would also know. What exactly was their game, and where exactly were they now? Strongbow wasn't an idiot either, so he would have some kind of backup just in case they were discovered, or would he? Perhaps a quick action of Trent's part could save the situation, maybe even win Strongbow over, although his family was never given to monetary persuasion. All of these thoughts ran through Andrew Trent's head as he looked at the coin.

"Monroe, I need to make some calls that it would be best that you don't know about," he said to the Goliath standing near his desk.

"Yes Sir, Mister Trent," Monroe answered and stepped out of the office.

Trent took a burner phone out of his upper desk drawer and called the only number in its directory.

After two rings the call was answered, "Hello."

"Is this Maxine's place?" Trent asked.

"You have the wrong number," the other end said.

Trent hung up and waited. In just a few seconds the burner rang again, this time from a different number and area code.

"Trent here," he answered, "I've got a job that has to be done tonight."

"Okay, where do you want to meet?" was the reply.

"In Middlesboro at the usual spot," Trent said.

"One hour," the phone went dead.

"Monroe, I'll need the car" Trent called to Monroe as he got up from the desk.

The man stuck his head back in the office, "Right away, Sir."

Trent headed out of the office and to the elevator for the short ride to the ground level. If he could pull off this plan, all his years of scheming and skullduggery in Washington would pale in comparison, but first, he had to know the location of that cave. Monroe had the limo started and the rear door open when he arrived.

"We need to be at the 'Back Door' Monroe. No hurry, we've got an hour," he told his bodyguard and then turned on the television to catch the local news that was reporting the story about finding George Simpson's head. He shut it off and stared out of the window, hoping nothing else would remind him of how badly the day was going.

## CHAPTER 16

"Angie, I'm going to go stir crazy if we have to sit in this room all day. Let's go get some Italian for lunch and then hit that Wal-Mart over in New Tazewell," Abigail said.

"The boys will not be too happy with us leaving while they're gone, Abigail. They both were pretty adamant about us staying in today," Angie reminded her.

"Oh pooh, they are both control freaks and you know it. Let's just go get a bite and then to Wal-Mart for some girl stuff that I need. What could be the harm? Nobody knows us over here anyway," Abigail argued.

"Oh all right, you win. I'm game for some Italian, besides, it will be a nice change of pace," Angie relented.

They found a small family run Italian eatery on the highway, and spent an hour with a fresh baked Lasagna before heading to the Wal-Mart for another two hours and then back to the motel. The short trip did wonders for their attitudes after the stress of the past few days. They were still laughing at some of the things they'd seen as they turned the key in the lock and entered the room. Angie was the first to realize that they were not alone.

"RUN ABIGAIL, RUN," she screamed, but it was too late, and another stranger pushed Abigail into the room, knocking them both off of their feet.

"Ladies, my friend and I are going to take you for a little ride. I can promise you that you will not be hurt if you don't attract attention by making a scene. If you do, I can promise that you will be hurt, but that you will accompany us anyway, understood?" the tall muscular man by the bed spoke softly.

Angie slowly stood up and then helped Abigail to her feet, "What do you want with us?"

"Actually, we don't know. Our job is to take you with us and wait for a phone call," he replied.

The one that pushed them into the room had an evil, soulless look in his eyes, and Angie knew there would be no mercy from him if they didn't obey.

"Okay, we'll go quietly," she told them.

They were ushered out of the room and into a dark Yukon that was waiting with the engine running. Whatever was going on, Angie suspected that it had something to do with the silver cave that Tom and Bob had found. Blindfolded and then sandwiched in the back seat between two other men as evil looking as the first two, the women lowered their heads and prayed as they were taken to Motch, Tennessee to a remote cabin. Not a word was spoken as the men removed their blindfolds and ushered them inside. Two of the men stayed inside with them while the others sat on the porch. Whatever was going on, the women knew that they personally would have very little to do with the outcome.

"Well, ladies, this is home for a bit so make yourselves comfortable. You will find that the place is escape proof and it has been thoroughly checked for anything that you could use to get out. You are free to roam around as much as you like, there is some water in the fridge, and the bathroom is over there. We will be outside until this is over with," the first man said as they left the large main room.

"Angie, I'm so sorry that I talked you into going out of the room," Abigail sobbed.

Angie put her arms around the older woman to give her comfort, "That is perfectly all right, Abigail. Those men found us at the room, and it wouldn't have made any difference if we hadn't left it. Besides, we had a great lunch. Just think of being stuck here with nothing but cheese crackers on our stomachs."

Abigail laughed at that and perked up, "Do you think that Bob and Tom know yet what has happened to us?"

"I think that whoever these thugs are working for will tell them very soon, but, Abigail, if this is about that silver, they are not going to let any of us leave here alive. We need to at least make it more difficult for them to kill us, don't you think?" Angie asked.

"I'm so frightened, Angie. Bob is much better at this than I am. After the problems that we got into because of the cougar in South Carolina, I promised myself that I was never going to go through that kind of stress again. Now look at me, and just after my mother's funeral too!" Abigail told her and started crying again.


Bob pulled the rental up to the motel room just after dark, "Tom, wasn't the truck in this parking place when we left?"

"It was, Bob. I'll bet the girls went out after we told them to stay put. I can't really blame them, though. I wonder why the room is dark?" Tom spoke.

They opened the room to see Angie's purse lying on the floor with the contents spilled, and Abigail's on the luggage stand.

"Something's wrong, Tom," Bob told him just as the room phone rang.

Tom rushed to pick it up, "Hello?"

"Mr. Strongbow, as I'm certain that you've noticed, your wives are not in the room. I can assure you that they are unharmed and will remain that way as long as you co-operate with me. Do you understand?"

There was something familiar with the voice although it was being filtered through something, a handkerchief maybe.

"I'm listening, what do you want from us?" he asked.

"Information, Tom, just a little information, and if I get it, you get your wives back unharmed," the voice said.

"What information?" Tom asked although he already knew.

"I want to know the location of the cave that the silver cob that you gave to Milton Bunch was in," it said.

"Is Mr. Bunch all right? Did you hurt him?" he asked.

"Not a bit. I do have the silver, though. Now, I want the location, preferably in GPS coordinates. Are you going to give them to me?" it asked.

"I don't have them. Bob Pike and I walked in and stumbled on the cave by accident. I would have to walk back in and retrace my steps," he lied.

"Then tomorrow morning I would suggest that you two go back to the cave. My people will be watching your every move. When we have the silver, you'll get your wives," the call ended.

"Did you hear that, Bob?" Tom asked, a little shaken.

"Yeah, I heard enough to know that neither you, I, nor the girls are going to come out of this alive if we give them the silver. If we go to the authorities with what we know, the girls will be dead. We're stuck between a rock and a hard place," Bob told him, "Let's get over to the office and see if the front desk knows who came in here this afternoon."

The night clerk was apologetic and wanted to call the police, but Bob explained to him the danger that would put the women in.

"Do you have a security camera running in the daytime?" Tom asked.

"Yes, ours are on twenty-four hours until we look through them. Follow me," he led them to the back room where the security monitor was located.

It took several minutes to bring up the video that they wanted, and, sure enough, there was the gray Yukon backed in to the parking spot in front of the room. As they watched the car pull out, Bob saw a perfect shot of the license plate.

"Freeze that right there!" he called out.

They couldn't believe what they were seeing. The plates were white government tags on an official vehicle!

"Holy crap, Bob. We've got feds on us for something!" Tom said.

"Maybe not, Tom, but we sure have somebody that works for the feds driving that SUV unless the tags are stolen, and that would be highly unlikely. Maybe these guys aren't as smart as they think they are," Bob replied.

They thanked the motel clerk and slipped him a twenty dollar bill to keep things quiet before going back to the room to think.

"What do we do now, Bob? I can't give them the silver or we are all dead if we don't give them the silver the girls are probably worse than dead. Have you got any ideas?" Tom pleaded.

"You know, I might just know someone that can help us out. I haven't seen him since my old partner's funeral, but this guy seemed to be connected somehow. The last thing that he told me was, 'If you ever need anything, don't hesitate to call'. I've kept his number in my phone ever since," Bob told him, "What have we got to lose?"

"While you call, I'm going to step outside and pray, Bob. Between that and your old friend maybe we'll get a miracle," Tom said.

Bob pulled the cell phone out and scrolled through the directory to Henry Albright's number. His hands shook as he realized that this long shot of a call was the only hope that he and Tom would ever see their wives again this side of Glory.

The phone rang twice, "Hello, Albright speaking." Henry answered the phone and Bob could feel a tear of relief trickle down his face.

"Henry, this is Bob Pike, Michael Tucker's old partner. I didn't know if you would remember me." Bob answered.

"Of course, I remember Bob! How are you and the Missus doing down there in Honduras?" Henry asked.

"Henry, Abigail and I have gotten into some big trouble during a visit to Kentucky, and I didn't know where else to turn for the kind of help that we need, "Bob spilled out.

"Whoa, slow down a bit Bob. Just what kind of trouble are you in?" Henry asked.

Bob told him about the hogs, the silver, and about Tom Strongbow. He also told him about the demonic activity that seemed to abound in the area and the fact that they were certainly going to be dead sometime in the morning if they couldn't get some help.

"All right, Bob, I might just be able to help, but we have to hurry. Give me the tag number off of that SUV, and I'll call you back in about thirty minutes," Henry told him, "Now relax. You are going to need your strength so don't waste it on worry. You've been through worse than this if I recall."

Henry ended the call and Bob decided that prayer was the best thing for him to do while he waited.

Outside, Tom was leaning on his truck with his head bowed over the bedside in prayer. He looked up to see Jeremiah standing on the other side smiling at him.

"Jeremiah, have you come to help us?" Tom asked.

"I've come to encourage you, Tommy. You are going through a trial of immense proportions right now, but there is a way out, The Lord has already provided it, all you have to do is have faith and be ready to act when the time comes," Jeremiah told him.

"Is my wife all right, Jeremiah?" he asked.

"They will be fine, Tommy, just be strong in your faith and remember that you are much stronger in your spirit man than those that oppose you," Jeremiah answered.

"Why didn't I see you for all of these years, Jeremiah?" Tom asked.

"Tommy, I've always been close by watching over you and ministering to your needs, that is my purpose. Now, you need me more, but soon, this will be over. You won't see me, but I'll still be there," Jeremiah told him and then faded like turning down a dimmer switch.

Tom went back into the room as Bob was getting off of his knees, "Don't let me interrupt, Bob."

"I was through. I'm waiting for a call back from Henry Albright and thought a little prayer couldn't hurt," he said.

"Jeremiah showed up and told me that the girls would be fine and that I was to strengthen my faith," Tom said.

Well, I have absolute faith that somehow we are going to prevail here, Tom. How about a cheese cracker?" Bob asked.

"No, I'm not hungry anymore, just frustrated about our situation," Tom replied.

"I feel better talking to Henry," Bob said, "There was a feeling that he had some deep-running connections when I met him, although he came off as just an ordinary guy. Maybe he can help."

The phone rang and Bob dropped it in his urgent rush to get the call, "Hello, hello? Oh hello, Henry, I dropped the phone," Bob apologized.

"That's okay, is your partner in the room?" he asked.

"Tom Strongbow is right here," Bob replied.

"Good. Put your phone on speaker and get something to write with. Now, because I was owed a favor by an Air Force buddy, I've got the location of that vehicle for you. It is close to a place called Motch, Tennessee at these coordinates, North 36.58 degrees and West -83.78 degrees. Now, it appears to be a single structure in some heavy woods, and there are four heat images outside of the cabin and two dim ones inside. I'm guessing those are the women. If these are government hired mercenaries, they are going to be armed, but probably won't expect you two to be coming after them. There may be an opportunity for a surprise if you can get to the cabin without being seen," Henry finished.

"We can find it Mister Albright," Tom replied, "I've got a Google Earth image of the location on my laptop."

"Well, be careful with that because it is not real time. I can help once you get there, but you need to step on it. The clock is running," Henry warned them, "I wish that I had more time to assemble a team, but they are several hours away from being any use to you men."

"Henry, I appreciate all that you've done. This gives us some hope, and that counts for a lot," Bob replied.

"Okay, keep in touch. I'll expect a call when you are close to the location," Henry ended the call.

"Well, I don't think the GPS in the truck is going to be much help on this run, but my Garmin might," Tom said as they walked to the vehicle.

"Two men with big game rifles against paid mercenaries, not much of a contest," Bob muttered.

"For them, you mean," Tom answered, "I'm planning on getting our ladies back if it means taking these guys on bare handed!"

"I just had a thought," Bob spoke up, "Head over to the Wal-Mart, I'm going to pick up some ear buds for my phone. That way I can listen to Henry without worrying about anybody hearing us talk."

"Somebody has been watching old spy movies," Tom replied, "but that is a good idea. I'll pick up a Tennessee road map too. Maybe it will give us a better picture of where we are going."

"Is that 1911 still in the truck?" Bob asked, "And how about a knife?"

"I keep that pistol in here, and I've got an old Kabar Marine issue plus a hunting knife that I carry," Tom told him, "Why?"

"If you are going to carry the Rigby, you need to have that Colt on your side for a little extra firepower. I need a knife for up-close and personal, if it comes to that," Bob told him.

"Let's get what we need and go get the girls," Tom replied.

They made the trip to the Wal-Mart where Tom picked up some camo face paint from the archery section along with a wicked looking Barnett BCR crossbow. He had no options except field arrows so he bought an extra six in a pack and met Bob at the front of the store.

"Whoa, a crossbow?" Bob asked.

"Yeah, I've wanted one of these for a while, but Angie wouldn't let me spend the money on it. Now I have a reason," Tom laughed.

"You know, that might just be the ticket to get us close to the cabin. Can you shoot one of those things?" Bob asked.

"Well, this one has an optic on it, so it is probably pretty accurate. The only problem is that we won't be able to check it out before we use it," Tom told him.

"They'll never see us coming," Bob laughed, "I just hope somebody makes a movie about this. It would be a real late night special."

"I'd bring the popcorn, that's for sure," Tom replied.

They headed the truck toward Motch in silence, each man with his thoughts of how the night would end.

## CHAPTER 17

Sheriff Daniel Ellis pulled into his driveway practicing the speech that he was about to give his wife, Susy about leaving Pineville for an extended vacation within the next few days. By extended, he meant that they were never coming back and their next major investment would be in tanning oil. He got out of the car and went to the front door just as it swung open suddenly.

"SURPRISE!" Susy shouted along with about ten other friends and family that had come by for the birthday party that she was throwing for him.

"What? I completely forgot that it was my birthday, Susy. You certainly did surprise me," he managed to hide his disappointment.

"Well, come on in, birthday boy. See who all turned out to wish you a happy birthday," she said taking him by the hand and leading him into the living room.

Everyone was shaking his hand and wishing him a happy birthday making this such a festive evening that he almost forgot that Johnny Simpson was dead. That was all brought back to him as someone turned on the TV and the evening news blared into the room.

"We have a breaking report from our CBS affiliate in Pineville, Kentucky on the death of a well-known sheriff's deputy, Johnny Simpson. His head was found by a Kentucky Wildlife officer, Joe Cloud this afternoon near Cannon Creek Lake, but the body is still missing. Authorities have still not ruled out an animal attack for his death." The national news anchor reported.

A hush fell over the room as everyone looked in Daniel's direction for a response.

"This has been an incredibly hard day for me folks, and as much as I appreciate this party in my honor, I'm not exactly in that mood right now. My apologies," Daniel told them.

They all filed out of the room after quietly relating their sympathies to the sheriff. Susy just stood apart from them and cried softly. After they were gone she sat by Daniel on the living room sofa.

"Why didn't you call me? I wouldn't have had the party if I had known," she said.

"It was late when they found the…ah…Johnny. I was really busy helping the fish and game people secure the site," he lied.

"Did he have any family in the area?" Susy asked.

"No, none that he talked about anyway. I think there was an ex-wife over in North Carolina. We'll have to check all of that out tomorrow," Daniel told her, "Listen, I wanted to talk to you tonight anyway before this came up. How about we take a long vacation, just the two of us and get away from here for a while. What do you think?"

"That's sweet that you want us to go, but you know money is a problem right now. I haven't worked in three months, and just having your income has left us a little tight," she told him.

"Well, pretend that money wasn't a problem. Could we go then?" he asked again.

"Daniel, even if money was not a problem, who would I get to stay with mother? You know that she counts on me to take care of her," Susy told him.

"I understand," he told her, "Listen, I'm worn out so I'll just go to bed early."

"But you haven't eaten yet." She told him.

"I'm not hungry." He said without looking back as he walked out of the room.

Andrew Tent sat back in the overstuffed leather chair with his feet up on the matching ottoman, smoking an expensive cigar and blowing rings toward the ceiling. After months of careful planning, he was about to pull off one of his grandest schemes.

"Monroe, are you ready for what we have planned for tomorrow?" he asked the bodyguard.

"Yes, Sir, I've got men ready to pack out the silver once those two fellows lead us to it. We'll kill them and put them in the cave with the bodies of their wives and then bring it down on them with a quarter stick of dynamite," he answered.

"What an exquisite plan, Monroe, even if I do say so myself," Trent beamed with pride.

"Yes, Sir, Mr. Trent," Monroe agreed, "What about the sheriff?"

"Daniel Ellis is no longer part of my plan, Monroe. Have you had any luck in finding that Johnson boy?" Trent asked as he got up to leave.

"No Sir, Mr. Trent, but his truck disappeared from behind the old man's place, according to a friend of mine that works over there," he replied.

"Well then, find the truck. How hard can a hot rod pickup truck be to find, anyway? Don't we have contacts in the highway patrol that we're paying?" Trent told him, "Get the word out and put a reward on any information that leads to him, but keep it quiet around here. I can't have his mother knowing that the little punk is still alive."

"Yes sir, Mr. Trent," the giant of a man answered.

Tom Strongbow pulled the truck over to the side of the road when Bob gave him the sign that they had a little phone service. The road they were on was between two ridges and the signal was cutting in and out.

"I'm going to call Henry. How close do you think we are, Tom?" Bob asked.

"We can't be more than a mile away, Bob, but I have a bad feeling about just walking in down this road," he replied.

Bob dialed Henry's number, "Okay Bob, I've been waiting for your call. You are about one-quarter of a mile from the cabin which is straight down that road and up what looks to be a drive about two hundred yards."

"How do you know that?" Bob asked.

"There's an MQ-1 Predator sitting up above you at thirty-five thousand feet or so, and he is keeping an eye on you for me," Henry answered, "Now we have a window so hustle up the road until you get close. From there you're going to have to be creative."

"Thanks, Henry, we're on it," Bob replied, "I'm leaving the phone connected so if anything changes, just talk into my ear."

"Will do, now get moving, and Bob, don't worry about making a mess in there, I've got a cleaner on standby,"

Tom set the Garmin to track the distance they walked, and then shouldered the Rigby and held the cocked crossbow in his right hand. He let Bob wear the 1911and his Kabar, and the two men set off at a fast walk up the dark road, leaving the truck pulled into the shallow ditch in case of any traffic.

They had slowed down to a careful stalk as the Garmin showed that quarter mile mark had just about been reached when Tom saw a small bit of light from the cabin shining in the woods at about two hundred yards.

"Bob, we probably need to sneak in from here, If I was one of those guys, I'd have my peepers on the driveway," Tom said quietly.

Bob nodded his head and checked the Remington to make sure it was ready as the two men eased off of the road and into the light brush along the edge which opened up after twenty yards. The ground had a covering of what felt like pine needles which aided their sneak in from tree to tree now that it opened up. They stopped after making the first one hundred yards without seeing any sign of the kidnappers. Bob pulled a small pair of Nikon binoculars from his pocket and glassed the area around the cabin. On the porch, two men were sitting in the dark except for a sliver of light from the cabin window which slightly illuminated them. He gave a signal to Tom and handed him the glasses. As Tom was glassing the porch, a stick snapped about thirty yards to their left, and both men eased flat to the ground and froze their movements. The one thing that concerned them was that these guys might have night vision equipment. If so, it was going to be a short night.

Tom eased the rifle to his side and positioned the crossbow so that it was pointing to his left. Between them and whatever made the noise, there was a large pine that was helping protect them from view but hindered theirs also. Whatever broke the twig was now moving at a diagonal to them and would cross about twenty feet in front. The sweat was running down their skin under their clothes and into their eyes, and the mosquitoes were swarming at every opening or thin cloth they could find, but the men didn't move, too much depended on it.

When it was just in front of them, but invisible in the dark with the moon behind a cloud, a match was struck revealing a man lighting a cigarette. The flash of the match looked like a bomb going off to Tom and Bob whose eyes had grown accustomed to the dark. As quickly and quietly as a rattlesnake striking, Tom was on one knee and firing the crossbow bolt directly into the man's face as the match illuminated it. As soon as he loosed the bolt, Bob ran forward to keep the man from screaming, but the arrow had caught the kidnapper squarely in the mouth and exited almost all of the way out of the back of his head.

As they took stock of the dead man's possessions, Bob reached over and unslung the H&K MP5 that the man carried. He quickly patted him for more magazines and found two, which he took. Tom tapped him on the shoulder and signaled for the weapon as he carefully leaned the Rigby against the tree. With a nod of his head, Bob handed it over and then turned to glass the cabin porch one more time. This time, there were three men on the porch with one standing close to their end.

"Tom, can you work your way around to the other side of the porch?" Bob whispered.

"Yep, what's the plan?" he replied.

"I'm going to get in a little closer and kill the one standing on this side that will distract them toward me so you shoot from your side. With any luck, we'll get them all, but be careful not to shoot directly at the cabin," Bob told him.

"Roger that, good luck," and Tom eased off into the dark.

Bob gave him five minutes to get into position and then started a careful stalk of the front porch through the pines, stopping to check on his target every few feet. At fifty yards, the moon came out from behind the clouds and gave an eerie look to the surrounding, but did little to light up the porch through the trees. Bob dropped slowly to his stomach and left everything on the ground beside him except for the Remington and the Kabar. Slowly, so very slowly he closed the ground between him and his prey until he could make out the silhouette of the man that he intended to kill.

Carefully, he slid the heavy rifle into position and just as carefully slid the side safety quietly forward. The open sights were next to useless in the low light so Bob sighted along the barrel toward the target. At this range the muzzle blast will kill him, he thought wickedly as his finger squeezed the trigger. Suddenly the moon broke out again and the sights wee somewhat visible., Wasting no time, Bob fired and the .375 launched the 300 grain Barnes solid toward the man at 2500fps and a little over 4, 000 foot pounds of energy!

Racking another round into the chamber, Bob found himself to be the target of the two companions of the man that he had just blown a large hole through who was now flopping on the porch like a dying fish. 9mm rounds were tearing up the dirt just in front of where Bob was lying, and he thought that he was going to get shot when a scream came from the porch which caused the man closest to Bob to swing around, giving him the perfect shot at the back. Bob hurried one down range just as a hail of bullets from the MP5 that Tom was carrying ripped into both of the men…and suddenly it was over.

Tom ran for the house and jumped over the slightly twitching bodies on the porch to get to the door. Bob was behind him slightly but stopped to remove the weapons from the dead and dying men before continuing in. His years of law enforcement would not allow anything else. When he stepped through the door of the cabin, there sat Abigail on the edge of the bed, watching Tom and Angie.

"Hey girl, I'm over here," Bob called.

Abigail jumped up and ran the few feet to him and threw herself at him, "I thought that they had killed you, Bob…all of that shooting and everything," she sobbed.

"Are you all right, Abby? They didn't hurt you?" Bob asked gently.

"No, they were actually fairly nice to us, although there was a hint that we were going to be dead in the morning," she answered.

Angie let go of Tom and came over to hug both Bob and Abigail, "It is so good to see you guys, but what took you so long?"

"Hang on a minute everybody, I forgot that Henry was still on the line," Bob signaled for quiet, "Yes sir, we've got them. Four of them down. Yes, sir, we are leaving now. Thank you so much."

"Wow, who was that, Honey?" Abigail asked.

"Henry Albright, dear. You met him at Tuck's funeral," he answered.

"Oh…"

"Tom, you need to wipe that MP5 for prints and leave it on the porch, and we need to pick up the Rigby on the way out. The cleaners will be here in fifteen so we have to move," He stressed the urgency.

They left the cabin with the women averting their eyes from the damage that the simultaneous impacts of both the .375 and the 9mms had done to the man by the door. Tom walked over to the one that had fallen off of the porch on his side and retrieved the bolt from his neck. He would have to get the other one in the woods on the way out.

"Tom, is that a crossbow you're carrying?" Angie asked.

"Well, I really needed it this time, Ang…I promise," Tom told her.

"Teach me to use it when we get home," she replied.

They made the walk to the truck in about ten minutes and were well on the way back to the motel when the cleaners showed up. By tomorrow there would be no trace of the men or the carnage.

The trip to the motel went by quickly, and Bob suggested that they not spend another night here, all things considered. They talked to the night clerk who happily arranged another location, one that his folks owned, and they set about moving their belongings over. Afterward, Tom insisted that they find someplace to eat.

"Abigail and I know this great little Italian place that is still open," Angie volunteered to the laughter of the group.

"Italian it is!" Tom decreed, but first I need for you to get that Mister Albright on the phone. I think we should give him the coordinates of the cave, after all, he probably saved our lives tonight."

"I'm all for that, Tom," Bob made the call while Tom dug the Garmin out and turned it on.

"Hello, Henry, I need to give you something from Tom and me as a way of saying thank you," Bob told him when he answered the phone.

"Well, Bob, nothing is owed to me for helping, but I do like gifts every now and then, "Henry answered with what sounded like a laugh.

"Have you got a pencil? I've got some coordinates for you." Bob said and then told him where to find the cave.

"My thanks to you both, and I'll make sure this gets to the right people," Henry told them before ending the call.

"Okay, we've given away a fortune, let's go eat!" Bob said laughing.

They would celebrate now and worry about tomorrow later.

## CHAPTER 18

The knock on the door just after dark startled Doris Hobbs who had been making a late dinner for herself and her daughter Emily, who had not yet returned home from her shift at the Dairy Queen in Pineville.

"I'm coming, I'm coming," Doris shouted before she opened the door and saw two men standing on the front porch, "Can I help you?"

"Yes, Ma'am, you can. I need to know where the person is that owns the truck in the garage," the taller of the two spoke first.

"I'm afraid that I don't know what you're talking about, young man," Doris replied.

The man's companion suddenly punched Doris in the chest, driving her back into the house where they quickly followed, shutting the door behind them.

"You're afraid all right, now tell us where to find Jimmy Johnson!" the taller man ordered while the other one pulled a thin bladed knife out from behind his back.

"Don't hurt me, please, "Doris begged, "I'll tell you everything that I know."

"Start talking then. My friend gets impatient easily," he told her, indicating the man with the knife.

"He is with a preacher named Josiah in Knoxville. That's all I know. I swear!" she pleaded.

"I need a number and an address," he said.

"The number that he called from is in my phone. It will be the only one with a Knoxville area code," she answered, weeping from fear.

The one with the knife spotted the phone on the kitchen counter and started looking through the call log. One number stood out almost immediate so he dialed it.

"Hello, Pastor Perkins speaking," Josiah Perkins answered.

The man hung up the phone and nodded to his friend.

"Now Doris, I can I call you Doris, can't I? If you tell anyone about our little visit, we will come back, and I'm going to let my friend there cut you real bad just for fun. Do you understand?" he asked menacingly.

Doris Hobbs just nodded weakly and lay on the floor crying. When she looked up, they had left with her phone.

The phone call that he had just received puzzled Josiah. He knew that the number of the caller was familiar but couldn't place it. He looked through his call logs for a clue and found the number of Doris Hobbs where he had picked up the Johnson boy. Alarms started going off in his spirit as he tried to come up with a reason for the strange call, but everything that he thought of bode ill for him and the boy.

The old man finished his small supper in haste and set off for the homeless mission where he had hidden Jimmy with the help of another pastor, not knowing that his every move was being tracked since he had answered the call from Doris' phone. The fact that the location of the mission was in one of the seedier areas of Knoxville didn't faze Josiah. He never left home without the little High Standard .22 derringer stuck in a waistband holster. While a man of strong faith, he also was a realist, and he was too old to take much of a beating or give one for that matter.

The drive to the mission took almost a half an hour to complete, and by the time that he arrived, the evening prayer service was in session. Josiah eased into the small chapel and sat in the back as the pastor led his small but growing flock in prayer. Afterward, he came directly to Josiah.

"Welcome, Brother, what are you doing over here at this hour?" Pastor Billy Jenks asked.

"I've got to see Jimmy Johnson, Brother Billy. Something has come up," he explained starting with the strange phone call.

The one thing that was now working in his favor was that Billy had been a police officer in Los Angeles for fifteen years before turning to the Lord and going into ministry. He had come to Knoxville three years before to get away from the West Coast and had not been there long when the tremendous need for a homeless outreach stirred him to action. Now his old police instincts kicked in as he digested what Josiah was telling him.

"Have you got that phone with you?" he asked Josiah.

"Why yes, it's right here," Josiah answered and produced the phone.

Billy took the phone from his hand and called another man over.

"Manny here will take the phone for a ride and drop it a long way from here. They are probably tracking its location even now" he said as he handed the phone to Manny and gave him his car keys.

"You need to leave with the boy, Josiah. I can stall whoever shows up as long as need be to give you a head start. My suggestion is to take him back home to Pineville and do it tonight. God speed to you," Billy told him.

"Bless you, Billy and thank you for helping with the boy," Josiah replied.

"It is my job, my friend," Billy gave him a hug and left the room as another man brought Jimmy in.

"We need to go, Jimmy. I'm taking you home," Josiah told him.

"Can I really go home, preacher? I'm in a lot of trouble back there," Jimmy told him.

"The Lord has made a way Jimmy. Trouble is one of those things that never looks as bad when you are looking back on it. This is going to pass. Now, come on, we've got to go," he told him.

They got in the old Ford and headed out of the area well ahead of the car with the two thugs that had roughed up Doris Hobbs. Those two got out of the car and walked into the mission where they were met by Billy Jenks who stood a head taller and somewhat heavier than either of the men.

"We are looking for Jimmy Johnson," the leader said.

"Doesn't ring a bell with me, son. What does he look like?" Billy asked courteously.

"Look, we know that he is here. A preacher named Josiah Perkins brought him in a couple of days ago. Now you need to let us have him," the man started to threaten.

Billy's face didn't change from the smile that he had on his lips when he delivered a thunderous overhand right straight to the bridge of the man's nose, shattering cartilage and breaking blood vessels. The man fell backward like he had been poleaxed in a slaughterhouse while his demented friend reached for his knife. That action was met by one of Billy's less mentally stable wards thumping him behind the ear with a large brass candle holder.

"Good work, Simon. Let's duct tape these boys in the front row of the chapel so I can preach to them for a bit before the police get here," Billy laughed while rubbing the tender knuckles of his right hand.

Simon just laughed, showing off the black stumps of his meth rotted teeth, "Praise the Lord, Pastor."

"Yes, Simon, Praise the Lord indeed!"

## CHAPTER 19

Just before midnight, the phone in Andrew Trent's desk drawer rang twice and then  went silent. Trent was just getting ready for bed when his personal cell phone rang, and he took the call in the upstairs hallway.

"Hello Monroe, I assume that you have good news to report," Trent aid.

"No sir, Mister Trent. The two men that we assigned to find the boy are in jail down in Knoxville. Apparently, a preacher beat them up pretty badly," Monroe reported.

"Hell's bells, Monroe. Can't your people get anything right?" Trent ranted, "Do you have any idea where the boy is now at least?"

"No sir, we had the preacher's cell phone tracked that took him down there, but that ended up in a beer joint across town, and Knoxville is a big town," Monroe told him.

"Keep looking then. It is imperative that we get that boy back before morning!" Trent hung up muttering to himself, "What else could go wrong?"

His phone rang again, "What in the hell is it now, Monroe?"

"Trent, where are my men?" came the voice on the other end that was not Monroe.

"How did you get this number? You know that you are never to call me at home!" Trent told him.

"The team that you hired is missing without a trace and the vehicle that was assigned is back in the motor pool. We need some explanations and we need them now!" said the person on the other end.

"I'll get them for you; just give me time for Pete's sake." Trent hung up.

Something had gone very, very wrong with his perfect plan, and now Senator Andrew Trent, once one of the most powerful men in Kentucky was on the verge of panic. His mind concocted at least a dozen exit strategies before settling on one that seem like it would be fool proof. He had received almost three million dollars as good faith money from the ten million that Milton Bunch had borrowed, and that was in the safe in the office. He could go there right now and get the money, make the run to Knoxville where his plane was fueled and waiting and fly to anywhere for a few weeks until things settled down.

The plan seemed sound enough so he knocked on the bedroom door to wake his wife.

"What is it, Andrew," she answered groggily.

I need for you to get up and pack a small bag. We are going to Europe for a couple of weeks on vacation," he told her.

"Have you lost your mind, Andrew? I can't just pack up in the middle of the night and leave. What would the staff think?" she protested.

"Listen, darling, I'm in trouble of the kind that we just can't get out of, and unless you want to be picking food out of dumpsters for the rest of your life, I'd suggest that you come with me," he insisted.

"I have my own money, 'darling'. What do you think I did with all of the bribes that I took to get your favorable vote on so many projects over the years? You go ahead and run like a fool to Europe. I'm staying here, and I will file for a divorce the first thing in the morning," she threatened.

"You would divorce me after the forty years that I took care of you?' he sounded bewildered.

"In a heartbeat! Now get out!" she ordered and locked the bedroom door behind him.

Trent made his way to his bedroom at the other end of the hall and threw some essentials into a small handbag. He had two spare suites on the airplane and several changes of shirts, underwear, etc. He next called the hanger where the plane was being stored and ordered it pushed outside and readied for immediate departure. The next call was made to Monroe.

"Monroe, I have to leave. How long would it take you to pack for a trip to Europe?" he asked.

"About thirty minutes, Mr. Trent," was the simple reply.

"Good, pick me up at the office in thirty minutes. I'll walk over there," he ended the call.

Andrew Trent left the house that they had lived in for the past twenty years without looking back. The three million would guarantee him a fresh start and the money to back a few lucrative hustles, something that he had gotten very good at. The walk to the office took all of five minutes, and soon he was turning the key in the lock for the last time.

Trent left the overhead lights off since the small desk light that was always burning gave him enough illumination to see the safe on the other side of the room. He quickly worked the dial to open the safe and then retrieved the briefcase with the money.

"Hello, Andrew," said a familiar voice in the shadows on the far side of the room.

Trent jumped in fear, "Oh, hello Milt, you startled me."

"Andrew, Andrew, Andrew, you have really disappointed me," Milton Bunch told him, "I was just getting ready for bed when one of my people called from the airport and told me that you had ordered your plane readied for immediate departure. Now why in the world would you do that?"

"Milt, I can explain everything. The silver deal has been compromised and I've got to leave," Trent told him.

"With my money, Andrew?" Milt asked quietly.

"Milt, I swear that I was just on my way to bring this back to you," Trent told him.

"You know, Andrew, I always really thought you were a crook, but one that was useful to me and my operation. Now that time of usefulness is over, and it is time to split the sheets...so to speak," Milt said.

He had been busy with his hands while he was talking, but Trent was too frightened to notice. Now Milton Bunch lifted a small Beretta 21A with a suppressor attached and shot Andrew Trent twice in the middle of his forehead. Milt then got up and walked over to the twitching body and emptied the magazine of the .22 caliber pistol directly into the back of the man's head before picking up the briefcase and walking out, closing the door behind him. He took the stairs down to the first floor and then a side door to the parking area where a car was waiting for him.

"Where to, sir," the driver asked as he opening the back door.

"Take me home, Monroe. You can have the rest of the evening off," he replied.

"Yes sir, Mister Bunch, Monroe answered.

Daniel Ellis had just laid down on the bed with his clothes still on when his cell phone rang.

"Sheriff Ellis speaking,' he answered.

"Sheriff, there has been some kind of disturbance in Senator Trent's office. You need to get over there," a voice said.

"Why don't you call the Pineville Police? Disturbances are their jurisdiction," he complained.

"Not when it comes to stealing silver it isn't," the phone call ended.

Daniel felt a cold sweat break out as he almost had an anxiety attack. He hurriedly put back on his shoes and started for the door.

"Where are you going, Daniel," Susy asked, "I thought that you were tired.

"I am, but I got a call. I'll be back in a little while," he told her.

Daniel made the drive over in a matter of a few minutes and took the stairs to the floor that Trent's office was on. He carefully opened the stairwell door just in case there was a trap laid for him, but saw nothing except the light from Trent's desk shining through the frosted glass of the window in the door.

He walked to the door and slowly turned the handle, surprised that it wasn't locked. There on the floor in the front of the open safe lay Andrew Trent, a pool of bright red blood under his head and the silver hair matted with it. Somebody wanted to send Daniel a message, and it wasn't lost on him. He walked to the desk and used a handkerchief to pick up the phone to call the police. After the call, he sat on the edge of the desk and waited for the officers to get there. He could explain a tip very easily to brothers in law enforcement, but how was he going to get the silver out of the cave now, and who would pay him for it? His cell phone rang and shook him out of his thoughts.

"Sheriff Ellis," he answered.

"Did you find him?" the voice asked.

"Who is this?" Daniel demanded.

"Sheriff, we know about the dealings that you had with Trent, and we also know about the trouble that you've faced trying to get that silver out of the cave on Cannon Creek Lake. I have a proposition for you," the voice told him.

"Go ahead, I'm listening," Daniel answered.

I have five million dollars in cash for you on the delivery of that silver if you can get it out of there without being seen. Does that sound like a good deal to you?" the voice asked.

"There is still the problem with the hogs and the publicity to contend with. Once that is handled, I can get the silver," Daniel told him.

"Write down this number and call it as soon as you have the silver in your possession, 555-6457," the call ended just as the police came into the room.

Although the rest of that evening until well after midnight was spent in the office of the late Andrew Trent helping the police gather anything that could be used as evidence, Daniel went home in a good mood knowing that he was still in line for a big payout when the silver was recovered, and his problems with Tom Strongbow and Bob Pike would end early in the morning. He slipped into bed without waking Susy and soon was in a deep dreamless sleep.

In the Pacific Northwest near the town of Newport, Washington, a bear of a man sat in his recliner and dialed the number of his trusted business manager in Miami, Florida.

"Good evening, Henry, what's the occasion?" Shaun O'Brien answered.

"Shaun, I'm sorry to trouble you this late, but something has come up. Can you assemble the team for a late night bag and extract tomorrow night in Pineville, Kentucky? Standard pay and a healthy bonus, of course," Henry told him.

"How many men do you need, Henry? I've got Tuck and Amos with me, and we can leave in a couple of hours," Shaun asked.

"The three of you will be all the manpower required, but we are going to need to transport almost sixteen thousand pounds of cargo out of there. I'll get your thoughts once you are airborne," Henry told him.

"Ten-four, Henry, I'll be in touch" Shaun ended the call.

Shaun O'Brien was a big man at six feet two inches and two hundred and twenty pounds. Age had started to catch up with him a bit at sixty-two, but he still had the physical agility and strength of a twenty-year-old. His physical prowess plus years of service with the C.I.A. and various other clandestine groups made him a natural for Henry's relatively new business as a 'Fixer' for almost any type of problem from domestic violence to international terrorism where an iron-fisted solution was necessary, and when Henry called, Shaun knew that there were no restrictions on what tactics to use for that particular job.

O'Brien's main team usually consisted of six men, but tonight he would call on two that had become like family to him, Michael

(Tuck) Tucker, and Amos Whitehorse, O'Brien's son-in-law and also the company hot-shot pilot.

Shaun left the main cabin of the converted one hundred and twenty foot Swift crew boat that he had turned into a luxury yacht. The three turbocharged 12-71 GMC diesels gave him a 22-knot cruise when he had to make an island run, but the boat rarely left the dock anymore due to the access they had to the new Antilles 21G Super Goose seaplane that Henry had provided after the last job in Texas.

He made his way to the forward staterooms where his pilot Amos was staying with his wife Maggie while they were in town, "Amos, I need to talk to you."

"Coming, Dad," a groggy voice answered through the door.

Amos opened the door, "What's going on, Shaun?"

"I need to get the Beechcraft ready to make a run for Knoxville, Tennessee tonight. We've got a job," Shaun said, "and quit calling me 'Dad'."

"Okay, Father, I'm on it," Amos answered with a grin.

"It's a good thing that Maggie loves you or so help me…" Shaun started, but the door closed.

He made his way to the aft living quarters where Tuck was staying with his wife, Hanna, and their two children before flying back to Barbados and the relative safety of their life under the aliases of George and Stephanie Alexander, Hanna's choice.

"Tuck, I need to talk to you, "Shaun whispered through the door to keep from waking the children.

Tuck came out of the stateroom into the companionway, "What's going on, Shaun?"

"We've got a 'bag and extract' up in Pineville, Kentucky tomorrow night. The old man says it carries a hefty bonus," Shaun told him.

"Let me tell Hanna. How long will we be gone?" Tuck asked.

"Plan for two nights, Hanna can stay here with Maggie and fly out when you get back," Shaun answered.

"I'll grab my gear," Tuck said as he went back into the stateroom.

## CHAPTER 20

Tom and Bob headed back to the lake well before daylight to give themselves time for a light breakfast. When they pulled up behind Joe's truck, the cruiser belonging to the sheriff's department was already parked in the road.

"Good morning, Tom, Bob," Joe said as they busied themselves unpacking the rifles from the back seat, "That's some serious stopping power Tom, are you looking for an elephant this morning?"

"I saw how slow they were to drop with a .556 the other day, and those were smaller hogs than the one we want, Joe," Tom replied, "Remember what we talked about yesterday, I need to wound the hog so we can take care of the demon problem before we kill it."

"I saw those hogs' eyes last night, Tom, and I am more inclined to believe what you told me this morning," Joe replied quietly so the others wouldn't hear him.

"Bob will handle the exorcism, Joe; just don't let anyone around that hog once we shoot him just in case they aren't protected. It would also be best for anyone in the area to keep their hands over their mouths and their eyes averted if possible," Tom said, "Where is the sheriff?"

"He was here just a minute before you showed up; maybe down at the end of the road," he replied, "Here come the dogs. Stand by at the edge of the tree line up there."

The dogs that the men brought to hunt had Kevlar neck and chest protection and were eager to get on with it. Tom was surprised to see a very large Great Dane with full frontal armor leading the pack with his handler.

"Bob, look at what they are using to run these hogs," he pointed.

"I heard that those dogs were originally bred to hunt hogs in Europe. This should be interesting," Bob replied as he loaded three down and one in the chamber of the Remington .375.

Joe directed the dog handlers to the area in the trees that he saw the hogs last night, and the two Black and Tan Hounds opened up almost immediately followed by a cacophony of sound as all ten of the dogs picked up the scent.

With a nod of his head as a signal, the dogs were turned loose to begin the chase and the pack soon could be heard from several hundred yards in front of the hunter. Suddenly, the baying turned to yelping and then silence. As the men waited nervously for word from the dog handlers, first one dog and then another ran silently passed them and back to the trucks.

Tom turned to Bob and yelled, "COME ON!" and started running toward the last position that they had heard the dogs.

As they came over the crest of a small hill, the dog handlers were standing over something on the ground, and the dogs were milling around silently with their tails between their legs.

"What is going on, men?" Tom asked.

"Take a look for yourself, mister," one of the handlers stepped back to make room for him.

On the ground beneath a large oak were the badly torn remains of what appeared to be two men. Bob came up just as Tom turned away from the sickening sight.

"That is the work of the hogs, Tom. It looks like there are two bodies there, or at least enough parts for two bodies," Bob spoke.

Joe came running up with Daniel Ellis right beside him, "I've never seen anything like this. Does anyone know who these men are?"

"The one is George Riva. I don't know who the other might be, but it looks like they were together," Daniel lied.

"That's my shotgun on the ground there, Sheriff. Now how do you suppose that Riva got his hands on it?" Tom asked angrily.

"I don't know Tommy," was all that he replied as he stood staring at the second member of his team to be killed by the hogs in one week.

"This just happened before we came in here, Tom. That means that the big hog is close by, and I think that we should continue to track him," Bob said.

"Are you guys nuts?" Joe asked, "These hogs just dismembered two men and you want to go after them?"

"If we don't stop them, or the leader of the herd, this will continue. These animals have no fear of man so that is now going to be their primary food source. I've had to make these tough choices for years, Joe, it was my job then, and it is your job now. You need to man up," Bob told him sternly.

"I'm going with you," Daniel spoke up.

The dog handlers were leading their terrified animals out of the woods.

"I think the dogs sense what we are after, Bob," Tom said as he broke the breech on the Rigby and check that two shells were in the chambers. He also hooked two between the fingers of his left hand in case he needed four rounds, "Sheriff, since you are the senior law enforcement officer here, how about walking in front of me?"

Bob gave him the nod and they started off toward the lake following the tracks of the herd but paying careful attention to largest hoof prints. Joe sent two men back down to the landing just in case the hogs tried to circle back through the trucks, and also to send in the medics to retrieve Riva's remains. Suddenly, Tom saw another person walking just in front of him but behind Daniel.

"Jeremiah?" he said quietly, "What are you doing here?"

"The others can't see or hear me, Tommy. I'm here to keep him from hurting you," Jeremiah said.

"Are you talking about the hog?" Tom asked.

"No, the animal won't be a problem much longer. The one that is inside will be, I'm afraid. You are going to have to be strong in your faith, Tommy," Jeremiah said.

"Where is he?" Tom asked.

"Did you say something, Tom?" Bob asked from beside him.

"Jeremiah is here, and so is the hog, I think," Tom replied without taking his eyes off of Jeremiah.

Jeremiah stopped and pointed to what looked like a large pile of boulders surrounded by heavy cover, "He's in there!"

"DANIEL!" Tom hissed, "Get back here, the hog is in front of you!"

Daniel Ellis turned to face Tom at his warning just as the huge hog burst out of the heavy cover straight at his back. Tom fired the .416 twice in rapid succession as the heavy recoil allowed and as the two 400 grain projectiles entered the chest of the animal with a combined energy of almost ten thousand foot pounds, the hog somersaulted and slid right up to Daniel's fear frozen back.

The other hogs broke out and tried to escape, but Bob dropped two with the .375 while Joe worked the bolt on the Remington 700 as fast as most automatics will cycle. Two of the hogs got away and Bob ran to the monster that lay unmoving on the ground, but it was too late, the hog was dead, and the demons had gone. The question was, where?

Tom was still standing with Daniel Ellis between him and Bob with Joe standing a few feet to his right shoulder. Jeremiah was still strangely visible to Tom and slightly to his left hand.

"Tommy, you must do this now!" Jeremiah insisted.

"JEREMIAH!" came a roar of rage from the mouth of the sheriff.

Tom said to Joe, "Pray like you've never prayed before," and then nervously, "By the power given to me by the Lord Jesus, I bind you from any further action, demon!"

"Puny Christian, I am not afraid of you! We are many in this body!" Turel spoke through Daniel.

Bob came closer to the man standing with an AR in his right hand and a horde of demons inside his mind.

"What is your name, demon?" Bob asked.

"LEGION, Christian," it answered.

"COME OUT OF HIM NOW IN JESUS NAME!" Bob commanded.

Daniel was thrown on the ground and started foaming at the mouth. Joe rushed over and got the AR out of his hand while Tom held him down.

"I SAID TO COME OUT OF HIM!" Bob commanded again.

Tom turned his head in time to see Jeremiah start glowing like an extremely brilliant white light. He had his arms outstretched as if worshipping the Lord.

The body on the ground started convulsing and his chest started heaving as if there was something living working its way out like a bad horror movie. Tom fought the urge to run and started praying instead. Suddenly it was over as Daniel gave a shrill scream and lost consciousness.

Jeremiah was still standing by Tom, invisible to everyone else as Joe called for the Emergency Medical Techs to come assist the sheriff.

Tom turned to him, "Why didn't that demon leave when I called him out?"

"Tommy, the demon sensed that you were afraid, and that killed your authority," Jeremiah told him, "but that is nothing to be concerned about, you will increase in strength to accomplish these things as you grow your faith. This will not be over unless the sheriff is protected by the Lord. Turel is roaming for a season, but since your friend did not send him to the abyss, he will return to his last home, be prepared," Jeremiah told him.

"Hey, Tom, come over here, I want to get your picture with this hog. Nobody is going to believe this without one," Bob called after the medical technicians carried the still semi-conscious Daniel out of the woods on a stretcher.

Tom walked over to straighten the hog's head up and propped the mouth open to show the deadly tusks which had just recently ripped two men to shreds. He then got behind it and proudly beamed as Bob took the picture which made the already immense animal appear to weigh two thousand pounds.

"Bob, send that to me so I can paste it on my lodge's Facebook page. That will give the guy's something to talk about," Tom told him.

"Yeah, but if they knew what we do about this hog, they probably won't go hunting with you anymore," Bob laughed.

"Demonic possession is hard for a Christian to believe, Bob, much less unbelievers. Why don't pastors teach this anymore?" Tom asked.

"Well, it is probably not needed to raise funds for the new family life centers and church additions. We were involved in the Baptist church for over twenty years and had no clue until we took that post in Honduras. That was sure an eye opener!" Bob replied.

I wonder if there are any more possessed animals roaming around like this one?" Tom asked.

"I honestly don't know, but it would certainly explain some of the rogue behavior of a few animals and a lot more men if there were. Let's get back to the landing, Joe will be wondering where we are," Bob said.

## CHAPTER 21

"Monroe, you need to keep that appointment with Mr. Strongbow this morning. It's kind of a shame really. I knew him as a young boy, and kind of took a liking to him," Milton Bunch said to the ex-bodyguard of the late Andrew Trent.

"Yes sir, Mister Bunch, I have two men out there that will follow him to the cave," the huge man replied.

"Monroe, did you hear Trent talking to the people that he ordered to kidnap the women?" he asked.

"No sir, he asked me to leave the room while he made the phone call, but I did drive him to the bar in Middlesboro to meet the contact," Monroe offered.

"Did you see the contact?" Milton asked.

"Yes, sir, I wasn't supposed to, but I kind of sneaked in to the back of the place while they met. He was about five-ten, slender build, close-cropped blonde hair, and a very light complexion," he told him.

"Excellent, you did a good job, Monroe. Now if you will go to the lake and oversee the details of today's operation, we will be almost finished with this project," Milton told him.

"Yes sir, Mister Bunch," Monroe said as he walked out.

Milton relaxed back in his chair and locked his hands behind his head. He was feeling confident that none of the people that Trent had called knew of his existence, which would be important to staying alive. Trent had recruited the help of one of the most dangerous men in Eastern Kentucky to take the wives of Tom Strongbow and Bob Pike, a man usually reserved for only the most clandestine operations and fully sanctified by the government in any assignment. With Trent out of the way, the women would still be dead, as would their husbands in a few short hours, and no one would ever know of Milton's double life as an upstanding senior citizen in his community and also an organized crime kingpin with ties to a powerful South American family.


"We are about thirty minutes out of Knoxville, Henry. Based on the load details that you gave me, and the location, we are going to need a CH-47 or the civilian version to hoist the cargo. Will it be ready for a pickup in the morning?" O'Brien asked.

"I'll make the necessary arrangements for the helicopter, Shaun, and I've got a crew in there now getting the cargo secured and ready for a lift. That will need to be trucked back to Miami and placed on the deck of your home until I can find a place to store it," Henry told him.

"Roger that, Henry. I'll call as soon as we secure the plane," Shaun replied and ended the call.

"Well, Tuck, there's part of the plan. I still don't have the particulars on who we are supposed to bag, but you probably are going to need body armor and weaponry or Henry would have sent a girl scout in to take care of it," Shaun laughed.

"We've got everything that we are going to need, Shaun," Tuck told him, "What's the cargo?"

"Almost seventeen thousand pounds of silver coins that were struck in the mid-seventeen hundreds," Shaun told him.

Amos just whistled.

There is something else that you need to know, Tuck. This operation involved helping two men, one of them is a professional hunter and guide from South Carolina, and the other is Bob Pike," Bob told him.

"You're kidding me!" Tuck exclaimed, "I can't believe that Bob is in Kentucky. I thought that he was down in Honduras pastoring."

"Apparently, he and Strongbow met up here while Bob and Abigail were attending her mother's funeral," Shaun told him, "I thought that you should know so you can avoid contact with him."

"Yeah, that has been hard for me since Bob was like my father while we worked together, but I also understand how important it is to keep my identity a secret. It has been a lot harder on Hanna," Tuck told him.

"That's why I figured that you'd want to know ahead of time…no surprises," Shaun replied and turned around in his seat.

"Amos, can you fly a CH-47?" He asked his son-in-law.

"Heck yeah, I can fly anything!" Amos Whitehorse answered with confidence, "What's a CH-47?"

Amos studied the look of shock on O'Brien's face for a second before saying, "Relax, Pop, I'm just kidding, of course, I can fly one of those birds."

"Boy, I'm going to drop you out of that thing if you can't. I just can't believe my daughter puts up with your crap," but he said it with a slight smile, and Amos knew that he was winning the big and dangerous old man over.

Shaun's phone rang again, "You're in luck! There is a helilogging outfit that has a hanger in Knoxville. I've made arrangements to rent one of their choppers for this job. The only drawback is that it is costing me twice the standard rate because we are supplying the co-pilot ourselves. Just remember that their pilot cannot know what this cargo is."

"Relax, Henry, my 'boy' can fly anything!" Shaun laughed.

"Okay then, pick the chopper up, and proceed to these coordinates: North 36.684 degrees and West -83.717 degrees. Once the load is secure, have Amos drop Tuck off up on Pine Mountain where you will pick him up. I've already rented a suitable vehicle for you from the Enterprise at the airport. Amos will return to Knoxville with the rest of the team members who are already on the ground, and they will transport the cargo back to Miami in a container that will be waiting at the helilogging company with the truck and trailer to move it," Henry told him, "Call me when they are on the way out, and I'll give you the rest of the details."

"Ten-four, Henry. We copy the instructions. I'll call when the cargo has been retrieved," O'Brien ended the call, "Well. Men, any questions?"

"We're good, Shaun, I'm just ready to get finished and get back home," Tuck told him.

"Aren't we all," Shaun agreed, "aren't we all."

The Beechcraft King Air 350i landed at the Knoxville, Tennessee airport, and Amos taxied it to the helilogging company hanger where the old, and well used, CH-47 was waiting with the rotors already turning slowly.

Parked next to the hanger was a new Peterbilt tractor with a short container loaded on a flatbed. Shaun got out and walked inside the hanger while Tuck and Amos walked to the helicopter and boarded. Amos went forward to the control deck and slid into the co-pilot's seat while the company man sized him up.

"Do much flyin'?" the man asked,

"F-16's mostly, replied Amos for effect, "with some time in Hueys and Harriers during the recent war, but now mostly just an Antilles Super Goose back and forth from the islands and occasionally that Beechcraft."

"Wow, F-16s eh? The older man asked, "I was always Hueys during the Gulf war, but I remember a hot shot fighter pilot named Whitehorse that took several hundred dollars off of me in a crooked crap game one night in Kuwait. What did you say your name was?"

"Jones, Parker Jones, and I'm real pleased to meet you, but I have to go check on my partner back there," Amos told him as he quickly got out of the seat and made his way to the cargo area.

Tuck and Shaun were standing in the side door talking when he got back to them, "Look here, that pilot knows me from Kuwait, and that's not good. I told him my name was Parker Jones so play along."

"Shaun laughed. "I've got to run. There's a ride waiting to take me to the rental, but I'll see you up there in about two hours give or take. Be careful with this cargo, Amos, and the boys that are riding it up. Tuck, please keep an eye on him."

"Yes sir," Tuck answered as Shaun jumped down and returned to the hanger, "Well, Amos. You heard the man, I'm now your babysitter. Go fly this bird."

Amos went forward and slid back into the co-pilot's seat, trying not to make eye contact with the pilot.

"Here are the coordinates," he said as he handed the piece of paper over without looking in that direction.

The whine of the engines grew louder and the rotors picked up rotational speed until the big bird lifted off of the paddock slightly nose down and began lifting. When they had gained the planned cruising altitude, the pilot turned once more to Amos and looked intently at him.

"Are you sure that you aren't Whitehorse?" he asked again.

"Are you kidding me with that again? Just fly this thing up there and pick up our cargo before I lose my sense of humor," Amos bluffed.

The rest of the trip was made in silence as they lifted over the Cumberland Gap and on to the Cannon Creek Lake coordinates.

Henry's two man team had been working at the cave since just after midnight, pulling the silver from the rotted leather sacks and worm-eaten wooden boxes, and putting it into heavy canvas bags that they had brought in for the occasion on two rental four wheelers. On the ground in the front of the cave was a heavily reinforced cargo net with a reinforced rubber liner now stacked with bags full of silver cob. The job was finished with about thirty minutes to spare so one of the men walked over behind a stand of oak to relieve his bladder. It was about this time that Monroe and the two thugs that had terrorized Doris Hobbs walked slowly in behind the man that was finishing the net rigging. They had been drawn to the sounds of activity coming from that cove after searching for Tom and Bob who didn't make it to the arranged meeting spot.

"Get your hands up and turn very slowly," Monroe told the operative while holding a Beretta FS on him.

The man did as Monroe ordered and turned slowly to face him as the smaller of Monroe's men slid his thin knife out from behind his back in anticipation.

Just as their eyes were all of the first man, the second came around the rocks behind them in silence and shot each one in the back of the head with a suppressed Beretta FS 9mm.

"Nice work, Jerry, let's see what's in the big one's pack," the first one said.

"Looks like dynamite and some fuse, some zip ties, and some duct tape. These boys were going to a party, Mike," Jerry responded as he emptied the pack.

"I'll bet that I know what the plan was for that dynamite. I think that we should put it to good use. Let's drag those bodies into the cave and bring the roof down. We need to hurry, the chopper will be here in a few minutes," Mike told him.

They dragged the three men into the cave and back in about thirty yards. When they came back toward the exit, Mike took the dynamite and placed it firmly in some cracks in the cave ceiling.

"Looks like about a minute on the fuses. Let's light her off," he said.

Jerry struck a match, lit the fuse, and they left the cave in a hurry. Shortly the ground trembled slightly as dust and a few rocks flew out of the cave mouth following the explosion. When they looked up from behind the rock that shielded them from the blast, there was no sign of the cave mouth except some rapidly settling dust.

"Good Job, Mike, and just in time. Here comes the bird!" Jerry pointed as he ran to the cargo net to receive the hook.

Both men rode the load to the chopper and up into the cargo hold where they spotted Tuck operating the winch.

"Hey, Tuck! Fancy meeting you here," Mike said.

"Hi Mike, Jerry. Did you run into any trouble?" Tuck asked as the bay doors closed.

"Well, I wouldn't have called it trouble exactly, but we were jumped by three punks, just like Henry figured," Mike said.

"Where are they, or shouldn't I ask?" Tuck smiled.

"They are in the lost Swift mine where I expect it will be at least another three hundred years before they are found," Jerry laughed.

Tuck got on the intercom, "We've got the load, head to the rendezvous and drop me off."

"Well crap, Tuck. I was looking forward to driving back to Miami with you and old Mike here, "Jerry told him.

"Not this trip fellows, I'm meeting Shaun for a little bag and extract cleanup tonight, and then we will be back probably tomorrow," Tuck told him.

"Well, we can see who gets to have all of the fun, can't we, Mike?" Jerry joked, "Keep the old man safe down there partner. Mike and I will be out next week for a little fishing if you can squeeze us in." Jerry told him.

"Anytime guys. You know that Hanna would like to see you, and the kids will be glad to see their favorite uncles. Plan on staying for a little while this trip. I've got to get on the hook. How about operating the winch?" Tuck asked as he hooked up his harness.

Soon he was on the ground with his kit at the location of the rendezvous waving off the chopper. Tuck moved his drag bag back into the bushes and settled down to wait for Shaun to show up.

The dust settled in the darkness of the cave where the three bodies lay in a pile. One of them suddenly coughed and moaned before sitting up and digging in his pocket for the led light that he had purchased for a dollar at the auto parts store the day before. He also felt for the thin knife that always adorned his belt before remembering that it was in his hand before the lights went out. Now he shined the small light over the bodies of Monroe and his buddy while trying to figure out just where he was. The bullet that had grazed his skull rendered him bloody and unconscious but not dead, a fact that was missed by Henry Albright's men in their haste to deal with the bodies before loading the silver.

Suddenly, he heard a different sound coming from further back in the cave, but out of reach of his light. He moved as far back against the pile of rocks that blocked the cave opening as he could and waited as the popping and grunting noises grew closer. Finally, in the wide beam of the dim light, he saw several sets of eyes shining, and the thug that prided himself on his skills with a knife, and who had never ventured very far off of the streets of Knoxville caught sight of his first hog. Just before the light finally grew dim and went out, he saw one set of eyes with a distinctly red glow to them headed straight for him.

The irony of his situation was lost on the punk in the initial moments of the attack when the razor sharp tusks of the demented animal slashed through muscle and cartilage just as his favorite weapon had done to so many victims, and, much like his reaction to his victim's torment, his ear piercing screams only served to spur the hog on.

## CHAPTER 22

"I think that we should say goodbye to the sheriff," Bob said as they walked out into the clearing where the search party had gathered.

"You know he had those men in there to kill us, don't you?" Tom answered.

"Yeah, but what better way to heap coals of fire on his head than to tell him that we don't hold a grudge, don't you think?" Bob replied

"I think that I'd like to throat punch that sucker for all that he's put us through, but I like your idea better. We'll leave him with a memory of our smiling faces which will live rent free in his noggin from now on," Tom laughed.

They walked over to the ambulance where Daniel sat with an oxygen mask over his face, and Tom stretched his hand out.

"We're getting ready to leave, Daniel, and I wanted to be the first to tell you that I forgive you for trying to have your men take us out this morning," he told the sheriff.

Daniel refused to extend his hand to Tom and only glared back at him. Bob stepped up and stretched his hand out also.

"Well, Sheriff, we got rid of your hog problem and those demons that have been the root of your problems, even if you don't believe it, but you need to go throw yourself on an altar and get your life right with God or they'll be back," Bob warned him.

Again Daniel only glared at the two men who turned their backs on him to go find Joe Cloud.

"Hey Joe, we're leaving in a couple of minutes and wanted to say goodbye," Tom called.

Joe walked over and shook each man's hand," I learned a lot about myself from you, men. Tonight I'm going to see my father who pastors a little four square church over in Middlesboro. He will want to hear about our encounter with the demons, and I could use his council after a lot of years," Joe told them.

"Joe, it has been a pleasure," Bob said as he gave the man a brotherly hug.

Tom followed suit and the two men walked to their car.

"I'm going to email those stealth cam videos to the Attorney General up here," Tom said, "Daniel needs to be brought up on charges."

"I agree, Justice needs to be served," Bob replied.

"What do you think that Henry will do with that silver, Bob," Tom asked as they drove out onto 25E toward Tazewell.

"From what little that I know about the man, he will probably find a way to help a few others out down the line," Bob replied, "Let's go pick up the girls and get a bite to eat before we have to leave."

"Anything but pork, I'm off of that for a while," Tom laughed.

Michael Tucker slapped at the three thousandth mosquito that tried to suck his blood since he had crawled back into the brush to wait for Shaun O'Brien to arrive with their car. The State park ranger had driven by twice, but was oblivious to his well-concealed presence, and Tuck heard them coming back up the long winding road just as he stepped out to stretch his legs. Instead of the State Ranger vehicle, around the curve came a ten-year-old Buick LaSabre with sun faded paint driven by a silver-haired old man that was slouched down in the seat.

Tuck's phone rang, "Where are you, Tuck?"

"Is that you in the Buick, Shaun?" Tuck answered.

"Yep, come on, I don't want anybody to see me pick you up," he replied.

Tuck grabbed his bag and jogged to the waiting car.

"What in the world…?" he asked looking around the car.

"What better than a car that ninety percent of the old folks drive around this area," Shaun told him, "Besides, we won't be in it long. The SUV that Henry rented us is back in Tazewell. I had a flash of brilliance and found this at a rent-a-heap lot on the way up."

"Who's the target, Shaun? Are we going to airmail him to Henry?" Tuck asked.

"He is a little-known drug kingpin named Milton Bunch that has been hiding in Pineville under the guise of a retired philanthropist. Knowing Henry, he is swapping this one out as a favor to someone that helped him on a job. We have to put him in the trunk and then deliver him to a gentleman from Interpol, who will fly him out of the country. Henry feels like our justice department would just take a payoff and let him go," Shaun replied, "We'll meet the contact just outside of Knoxville at the rest area on I-40 to make the drop, then back home to a little peace and quiet."

"Sounds good, although I would have liked to have seen Bob Pike again. Maybe someday," Tuck told him.

"Maybe," Shaun replied, "let's go scout the area and come up with a plan. Apparently, this Bunch character only has one bodyguard around part time since his cover has been built over the years. Who would guess that he is other than a retired executive?"

"Well, we are tanned enough to pass as tourists. Why not walk around town and take pictures? We can find a place to eat and see if any of the locals know Mr. Bunch," Tuck threw that out.

"We have a plan!" Shaun laughed, "Let's go hide the car in a parking spot somewhere."

"My thought exactly," Tuck laughed with him.

They found a parking spot jut off of Walnut Street downtown and across from the Flocoe Restaurant where a group of people was standing outside. O'Brien parked and the two men walked slowly up as if sightseeing. They were quickly close enough to hear one of the women in the group talking to the others.

"I heard it from the horse's mouth not two hours ago," she said to everyone within earshot, "That no good son of Ruth Ann's turned up out of nowhere last night with a story straight out of fiction about where he had been, and after having all of those folks thinking a hog had eaten him. Why I can't imagine what his poor mother must have gone through."

Everyone was nodding their heads in agreement and talking amongst themselves as Shaun and Tuck walked past and entered the Flocoe.

"Hello folks, can I help you?" a pretty teenager asked.

"A table and a couple of menus, young lady," Shaun replied, "Say, what is all of the fuss out there?"

"Oh, that is just Agnes Bunch stirring folks up with some news that she heard this morning. Most people just let her ranting go in one ear and out the other," she said, "Can I get you something to drink?"

"Sweet tea please," Tuck said.

"Same here. Who is the boy that she is talking about?" Shaun was all ears once he heard the name 'Bunch'.

"Oh, that is Jimmy Johnson. He disappeared a few days ago and everybody believed that he had been eaten by a hog over at the lake. He is a real jerk," she replied, "but he told his parents last night that he had found a cave full of silver out there on the other side of the lake, and that he and Deputy Simpson were there when the hogs killed him. He also said that the sheriff was trying to have him killed and a whole bunch of other crazy stuff. I'll get those teas."

Across the room towards the back, a table with several older people had been eating lunch, but they stopped and turned to stare at Shaun and Tuck while the waitress told her story. Now one of the men got up and walked over.

"Hi fellas, are you from out of town?" he asked.

"Shaun didn't particularly like the attention, but he remained polite, "Yes, sir, we are headed to Bowling Green to see some family and decided to stop in for a little historic sightseeing and lunch."

"We get a few visitors through here from time to time. Not so much anymore since the coal mines are shut down, but we don't see people with dark tans very often," he replied.

"Just flew into Knoxville from Miami Beach on business. We decided to go see our family and kill a little time before we had to go back, so I rented an old car and here we are," Shaun said but was suddenly suspicious of the questioning, "My name is Bill Jackson and this is my son Maynard. I didn't get yours."

"I'm Milton Bunch, Mister Jackson. Pineville has been my home for many years so I probably come off a little forward when I talk to strangers," Milton told him.

"Not at all, sir, not at all," Shaun said politely as he shook the extended hand, "It's good to meet you."

"Likewise, and what did you say your business was?" he asked.

"Antiques, Mister Bunch, Dad and I buy antiques and sell them to overseas markets," Tuck said quickly.

Shaun gave him a big smile, "You wouldn't have any nice pieces that you'd want to part with would you, Milton?" Shaun adopted a tone of familiarity.

The waitress came back with their tea and interrupted the conversation briefly to take an order of two hamburgers loaded.

"You know, my wife might have some things that you'd be interested in, Bill. She is just outside. I'll go get her and have her come back to talk to you, I'll be right back," Milton told him and walked off to get his wife.

"How about that, Maynard? Right into our laps." Shaun laughed.

"You couldn't come up with something besides 'Maynard'?" Tuck whispered.

Both men stood as Milton brought Agnes back to their table and made the introductions.

"Agnes, why don't you find out what these nice young men are looking for in antiques. I've got to finish my meeting and then I'll rejoin you," Milton said and walked back to the table with his friends.

"Please sit down, Missus Bunch," Shaun indicated next to Tuck.

"Thank you, Mister Jackson. There has been so much going on this morning, I'm in quite a tizzy," she started, "That Johnson boy has everybody headed to the lake to look for a lost silver mine, and the things he has said about demon possessed hogs and everything. You've never heard the like of it."

"I'm sure we haven't Ma'am, now what about some antiques?" Shaun asked.

"Well, I've got maybe six nice pieces that I could let go of if the price is right, but you'll have to come to the house and look for yourselves. They might not be suitable at all for your market," she replied, "I just can't get over that boy just waltzing back home like nothing had happened with all of those tall tales."

"I understand, Agnes. I had my troubles with Maynard when he was young, but he turned out to be a chip off the old block, as they say," Shaun smiled at the look on Tuck's face, "What time would it be convenient for you for us to stop by?"

"Well, I have to ask Milton to be there, of course. Avoid all appearance of evil and all that, you understand," Agnes replied standing to walk over to Milton's meeting.

"Of course, Agnes, we have a good bit of time before we have to be anywhere else," Shaun reassured her.

"My God, I'd pay someone to kidnap me if Hanna was like that!' Tuck leaned across the table and whispered just as the waitress walked up with their hamburgers.

"I know, right?" she whispered as if in a conspiracy with them as she sat the hamburgers on the table, "I would have run away a long time ago if she was my mother!"

Shaun and Tuck shared a good laugh when she had left and had just started on their burgers when Agnes came back.

"Milton says anytime after three this afternoon. Now I have to run, but here is the address," she handed a piece of paper to Shaun.

"Thank you, Agnes, we will be over after three," Shaun told her.

Tuck had taken another bite of his hamburger when Milton Bunch walked back to their table while his friends filed by and stood at the register up front.

"Bill, Maynard, I'll see you at three then?" he asked.

Shaun extended his hand, "Absolutely Milton, we are looking forward to taking a look at these antiques and possibly turning this into a business trip…deductions and all that."

Milton smiled and joined his friends.

Shaun finished his hamburger without looking up again, and Tuck just sat sipping his drink, the hamburger relatively untouched.

As soon as they crowd had filed out, Shaun asked, "Well, is that tingle back?"

"Yeah, something's wrong. I think we may be getting set up," Tuck replied.

"I feel it too. There is something about Milt that is making my stomach churn a bit. I wonder how much muscle he will have at the house when we get there?" Shaun said.

"Here's my thought on this. Let's blow off the antique shopping trip at three, and instead, make a visit after dark, say around ten tonight. We can drive by when we leave here, recon the surroundings and sneak in later," Tuck told him.

"I like it, finish that burger and then we'll walk around town a bit to keep the antique buyer cover before we drive over," Shaun agreed, "What have we got for firepower?"

"I've got two H&K MP5SDs. This wasn't supposed to turn into a shootout, but if it does, those will make it a bit more even," Tuck told him, "Plus my body armor. I assumed you would have yours with you."

"I do, but I want one of the H&Ks," Shaun told him, "Let's go look around."

Daniel Ellis got up from the back of the ambulance and took off the oxygen mask before walking shakily over to where Joe Cloud was standing with other wildlife officers.

"I'm leaving, Joe. If I can do anything else, call my office," he said.

"Are you sure you're okay sheriff? That was some nasty stuff going on in there," he pointed to the woods.

"I'm fine. What else happened while I was out?" Daniel asked.

"Well, a heavy lift chopper was working timber or something across the lake, but other than that, nothing else," Joe told him.

"Where, exactly?" Daniel asked, suddenly agitated.

"Just across that cove yonder," Joe pointed in the direct that the chopper was working.

Daniel turned suddenly and ran for his car. He spun it around in the clearing and headed for George Tuttle road. Someone had stolen 'his' silver, and the only ones that knew about it were the Johnson boy and Tom Strongbow. He got to where Monroe had parked the truck that he had come in with his men that morning and started off across the two miles of wood and rough terrain at a run. When he got to the cave entrance, he knew that his fortune was gone along with his dreams. Daniel sat down on a rock near the collapsed cave entrance and drew his Glock. Placing it under his chin, he tightened his finger on the trigger. At that precise moment of weakness and despair, Turel and his troop entered Daniel's mind and took control of his thoughts. The long nightmare had begun. Daniel dropped the Glock while trying to holster it and walked as if in a daze until he reached the patrol car.

Wave after wave of sickness hit him as spirits of depression and infirmity rooted themselves firmly in his mind while rage and hatred welled up inside. Daniel had lost control of his thoughts to the demons that had come back to find it cleaned after Bob had cast them out. Now he lay face down across the hood of his cruiser and slobbered while beating the sheet metal with his fists. He was in that position when the Kentucky State Police found him to arrest him for various counts of dereliction of duty and conspiracy to commit murder based on the videos that Tom had emailed to the state attorney general a few hours before. As they handcuffed the slobbering and sobbing Daniel Ellis and started to load him in the back of the Trooper's car, he started violently struggling, screaming, and cursing the two troopers that were arresting him. Finally one of them tased him into submission, and they threw him unceremoniously into the back of the patrol car.

"You can't hold us!" Turel screamed through Daniel's mouth, "We are LEGION!"

"Settle down, Sheriff. You'll be with friends shortly," one of the troopers turned to him, "Hey, he's got one of his hands loose!"

"Impossible!" the driver told him and adjusted the mirror so that he could monitor the prisoner, "Well, if he gets any more violent, tase him again."

At the threat of another round of tasering, Daniel settled down, and they drove him to the Pineville jail where it took six men to get him processed and into a holding cell.

## CHAPTER 23

Shaun and Tuck made the street corner and walked behind the Pineville City Jail, a magnificent old brick building that looked like it had been renovated, although the top floor still had a medieval look to the barred windows. In the back of the building, six uniformed men were trying to wrestle a reluctant prisoner out of a state trooper's SUV and into the jailhouse. Unable to physically restrain him after several attempts, three of the jailers simultaneously used tasers on him until he flopped on the ground.

"Well, we need to make sure that tonight goes off without a hitch," Shaun said as he pointed to the fracas, "I certainly don't want to spend the night here."

"I'll bet that fellow is sore in the morning," Tuck replied with a shake of his head, "If he had been holding a light bulb in his mouth, they'd have lit it up."

"Let's go for a drive," Shaun suggested, suddenly feeling uneasy at what he was seeing.

They retrieved the old Buick and drove to the address that the Bunches had provided. Milton Bunch might have given the impression that he lived in retirement austerity during his conversation with them, but the reality was that he had a very nice and very secure estate home that resembled an old Victorian with an octagon tower and steeple roof in the front over a large porch. The property was surrounded on three sides by a stone wall and had numerous trees inside of what appeared to be a white board fence toward the back.

"Well, that certainly doesn't look like Mister Bunch is starving by any means," Tuck observed.

"No it doesn't, but we need a plan for tonight, because I'll guarantee that he has either a killer alarm system or bodyguards, or both, and I don't want to leave a trail of dead bodies if we can help it," Shaun cautioned.

"Well, it's only two thirty. We could go on in and buy all of her antiques. How much cash did you bring?" Tuck asked.

"Probably about two grand. How much do you have?" Shaun answered.

"I travel light, Shaun, maybe a thousand," Tuck responded, "and I can't use my card because it doesn't belong to Maynard Jackson. Nice work there, by the way."

"I want to go on the record as telling you that I think this is a bad idea," Shaun said.

"Noted, but we've lived through worse ideas now haven't we?" Tuck laughed, "Park the car, Dad, and let's go buy some furniture."

Shaun parked the Buick on the street in the front of the house, and the two men walked up the long flight of cement steps to the sidewalk leading to the house. On the way, they passed a gardener that appeared to be trimming some fruit trees, but on his hip was a pistol in a tactical holster. That didn't go unnoticed by Tuck either. When they gain the porch, Shaun pressed the doorbell and was rewarded with a very distinctive, antique sounding bonging tone.

The door opened and a fairly attractive young woman greeted them, "You must be the Jacksons. Please come in, "Mister and Missus Bunch are waiting for you in the living room."

As they walked behind her, Tuck noticed the unmistakable bulge of a pistol that was stuck in the back of her slacks and hidden below a loose blouse.

"Ah, Bill and Maynard, we've been expecting you," Milton greeted them, "That will be all Lucy. I'll call when our guests are leaving."

"Well gentlemen, welcome to our humble abode," Milt told them, "Agnes wasn't certain that you would come, but I assured her that you would. Thank you for not disappointing us."

Shaun caught the menace in his tone, "Milton, Agnes, thank you both for your hospitality. We would like to take a look at those antiques that you mentioned. Maynard and I have to be in Bowling Green earlier than expected."

Milton looked at Shaun for a few seconds, "Of course, Agnes, show these men the antiques that you talked about."

They followed Agnes to an upstairs bedroom that was being used as a storage room and pretended interest while she showed them a quarter sawn oak dresser, a large fireplace mantle with spindles and beveled mirror, also oak, and several small mahogany tables all covered with sheets and protected from dust.

"Agnes, I think that I would be interested in the fireplace mantle and the dresser, if the price is right of course," Shaun told her.

"Well, I would have to get at least five hundred for the mantle and seven fifty for the dresser. How about the mahogany tables, Bill? Surely those would sell well in the islands," she said.

"Hmmm, mahogany pieces are plentiful, Agnes, but quarter sawn oak of that quality is not," Shaun had pulled ten, one hundred dollar bills from his pocket, "I'll tell you what. I'll pay you one thousand for the two pieces, and have someone pick them up next week."

She looked at his hand with the ten crisp bills in it, "It's a deal, Bill! Now if you need anything else, don't hesitate to come back by and see us."

"I surely won't, Agnes. Thank you for selling these to me," Shaun shook her hand after handing her the cash.

Milton just stood by and watched the transaction quietly before turning and walking back downstairs followed by Shaun, Tuck, and Agnes who was beaming over her gain on what she considered being junk pieces.

"Thanks again, Milton, we need to be going. I'll have a freight company over next week to box these things and ship them to us," Shaun told him.

"Where exactly is your company, Bill? I didn't get a business card," Milton had lost all pretense at being friendly.

Shaun didn't lose his smile. He stuck his hand in his pants pocket and brought out a leather card holder from which he extracted a very plain but upscale linen card in off white with black raised letters which said simply: Trade Winds Antiques. LLC and gave the P.O. Box for the business along with William Jackson, Proprietor, and his phone number.

"I'm so sorry about that Milton," Shaun said jovially as he handed him the card, "It slipped my mind."

Milton just stared at the card as Agnes showed the two men to the door. Somehow, his instincts must have been wrong about those two, but it wouldn't hurt to run a check on the business.

"Lucy!" he shouted and the woman came running out of the dining area, "Run a complete background check on this company and on William Jackson immediately."

"Right away, sir," she replied and trotted off.

"Well, that could open a can of worms, Shaun. What are you going to do if he runs a check on that company?" Tuck asked after they were back in the car.

"Tuck, the company is legitimate. William Jackson is an upstanding man with impeccable credentials that we keep on the payroll for just such occasions as this," Shaun told him, "If they run a check on the company, which they are probably already doing, they will find that Trade Winds is rated highly by the Dun and Bradstreet and that Mister Jackson has a pristine criminal record plus a credit score of close to seven hundred and fifty. Henry pays a lot of money for this service."

"Well, we have a few hours to kill, What is next?" Tuck asked.

"We need to drive back to Tazewell and drop this heap off. We'll pick up the SUV and check our gear. I didn't see any electronics in the house, but we know that at least two bodyguards are there besides Bunch, who I'm sure wouldn't hesitate to kill us if needed. How do you feel about killing a woman?" Shaun asked.

"I sure don't want to kill anyone, but it wouldn't make me hesitate if she were to attack," Tuck responded, "I think that we need to get in and out with no noise, and let them all wonder what happened to their boss in the morning."

"We'll need some chemicals for that. It's a good thing that I considered those options when I packed," Shaun told him, "I've got a CO2 dart rifle and juice of my own concoction in the SUV that will take care of any sleeping problems that they might be having. When Milt wakes up, he'll be on a private jet to Europe."

"If we are going to work the late shift, how about finding a joint to eat in after we pick up the SUV?" Tuck asked.

"Good idea. We can eat and still have time to let it settle before the late shift," Shaun laughed.

## CHAPTER 24

Tom Strongbow, Angie, Bob Pike, and Abigail decided to have an early dinner after checking out of the motel since the Pike's didn't fly out until a little after midnight. Tom and Angie wanted to get home to the kids, and both couples were drained from the activity of the past few days.

"Anybody else feel like pizza?" Tom asked.

"There's a Pizza Inn not too far from here, I saw it the other day when we went to Wal-Mart," Angie said.

"Pizza is fine with us too," Abigail chimed in.

"Pizza it is then," Tom replied, "We'll follow you over."

The conversation at the table centered on the unusual events of the days before, and how little modern Christians understood about demonic activity and such. They ordered a large pepperoni with extra cheese and sat for almost two hours in the quiet Pizzeria sharing insights with each other.

"Well, guys, we've got about a five-hour drive ahead of us so if we are going to get home before midnight, we need to go," Tom said as he picked up the check.

"I think we'll just sit here for a little while longer, Tom. There aren't too many places like this in Honduras and you kind of miss things that you normally take for granted," Bob told him as he stood to shake his new friend's hand.

Angie and Abigail hugged and wiped tears as they said their goodbyes with promises to keep in touch and then they were gone. Bob sat back down with his back to the door with Abigail on his right side. They had been through a lot together and had expected the last weekend to be a breather for them both. Now they were looking forward to returning home just to be able to get some rest.

"Bob, don't turn around, but those two men that walked in look oddly familiar. I know that we've seen them somewhere," Abigail told him in a whisper.

"How can I see them if they don't turn around?" Bob asked, slightly irritated.

"They're to be seated in a minute, you can look then," she answered, "Okay they are across the buffet island directly to your left. Get up and get some more salad and take a look."

Bob stood up and moved nonchalantly to the salad bar so he could see who these men were, but one of them had his back to the room, and the other was turned away, looking out of the window on their side. There was something familiar about them, though.

"Well?" Abigail asked when he returned.

"I couldn't see their faces, but they look kind of familiar. We probably know somebody back home that they remind us of with the tans and all," Bob told her.

"One of them is coming to the salad bar, Bob. Now you can see him. Oh my, God, that's Michael Tucker!" Abigail told him in an almost hysterical voice before she fainted.

Bob looked at his wife, and then at the salad bar. Sure enough, even with the dark tan and the bleached hair, he recognized Tuck was standing frozen in place just staring across the island at his old friend. By this time Shaun O'Brien had come around after hearing Abigail's commotion and took Tuck by the arm, leading him to Bob's table.

"Bob, we need to talk quietly," Shaun started so as not to alarm the other patrons, "Is Abigail all right?"

Bob turned to Abigail who was slumped on the table. He wet a napkin in a little ice water and touched it to her forehead to revive her.

"Abigail, wake up, Honey," Bob said gently without taking his eyes off of Tuck.

Abigail stirred and sat up, "Pastor Shaun, Tuck is that really you?"

"Bob, Abigail, this is going to be hard to hear, but you need to listen to me. We are both in a type of protection program because of things that started in South Carolina. You cannot tell anyone about us. Do you understand?" Shaun asked gently.

"Bob had tears in his eyes as he realized that the young man that he had felt so close to and recently mourned was still alive.

"Tuck, can you sit and talk to us for a little bit?" Bob asked.

"I suppose there is no harm in that now, Bob. It might even be the Lord that brought us to this small out of the way place at the same time," Tuck said.

Shaun waved to their waitress to tell her that they had moved.

"Bob, Henry told me that you were up here after you told him about the silver," Shaun said, "How have you two been? Is the ministry still going all right?"

"Shaun, we're doing well, and, yes the ministry is flourishing thanks to the foundation that you laid for it," Bob replied, "As a matter of fact, we have to catch a flight early in the morning back down there."

They talked about many things for the next two hours, and Tuck got the chance to tell them about Hanna, and the children, and the fact that it was so hard for them to leave their friends and family the way that they had to. Finally, it was time to leave.

"Bob, I've got a plane in Knoxville that we will be flying back to Miami in a few hours. I'd like for you and Abigail to fly back with us, and then I can have the company pilot fly you into Honduras when he takes Tuck and Hanna home. It would give you all a chance to catch up and to see Hanna again. What do you say?" Shaun offered.

"I think that we would love that. Thanks, Shaun," Bob replied after Abigail squeezed his hand.

"Stay close to the terminal, and I'll have you paged when we get back," Shaun told them.

Tuck hugged Abigail and Bob wishing that things had turned out differently than they had, but life is like that. At least they would get to spend a little more time together before having to put the cloak of secrecy back on.

"Well, that was nice," Shaun said as they got into the SUV.

"Mighty strange if you think about it, Shaun. What are the odds of running into them like that?" Tuck responded, "It was nice, though. Hanna is going to be surprised!"

They drove back to Pineville and arrived a just after nine pm. With the SUV not having been here before, they had a certain amount of anonymity if they didn't get out of the vehicle before dark, which was fast approaching with the town being situated in the between the tall ridges. Shaun parked well up the street from the house in a spot where the woods came all of the way to the road.

"Okay, Tuck, have you got the plan down?" he asked.

"Yep, I ease up behind the house and ice anyone that is outside, then I give you the all clear with the handheld and wait for you to get in position behind the house before I make entry through the front. We ice Lucy and Agnes if need be, and then we take Milt out and load him in the SUV...piece of cake," Tuck replied.

"Just don't get cocky youngster," Shaun gave him a smile. He knew that Tuck was the coolest hand under fire that he could have with him.

On a three count, Tuck rolled out of the SUV with the MP5 slung over his back and the dart gun in his hand. The 1.5cc syringes were filled with one of Shaun's concoctions that he hoped would prove non-fatal to the recipients. He made the short step up across the sidewalk and into the tree line as Shaun drove slowly away to park on the opposite side of the house in a relatively secluded area that was out of sight of the main street.

Tuck watched carefully for any signs of movement in the small orchard that his first target had been tending, but didn't see him. He decided to come out of the woods near the front side of a white picket fence that surrounded the orchard. As he crossed the fence quietly, something in the corner of his eye caught his attention. Tuck dropped to one knee and froze while he waited for the movement again. There it was. Someone had just lit a cigarette and was trying to shield the glowing ember with their hand about thirty yards from him.

"Don't you know that cigarettes are harmful to your health?" Tuck asked silently.

He needed to get ten yards closer so that the target would be at least silhouetted, so he crawled slowly and silently forward with the CO2 rifle charged and the night optic turned on a red dot.

The person smoking the cigarette suddenly stood and look past where Tuck was positioned as if he heard a noise. The next noise in the yard was the dull thump of a body dropping like a stone in the manicured grass. Tuck moved quickly to the gardener and took the pistol that was in his pocket along with the radio that fell beside him. After reaching over and pulling the dart from the man's neck, he moved toward the front of the house.

"We are go, repeat we are go," he said softly into the two way radio that he carried.

"Copy we are go, over," Shaun responded.

Tuck was kneeling in the shrubbery near the front door when the radio of the gardener went off softly, "Casey, come in Casey, is everything clear?"

It was the woman's voice and Tuck knew that he had to respond, "All clear."

Sweat was running down his face now, partly from heat and partly from nerves. If the woman suspected that he wasn't Casey, the party would be over before it started.

The radio came alive again, "Okay."

Tuck decided to make the move through the front door and swung up over the porch railing and started toward the front. As he moved across the porch, he noticed that one of the floor to ceiling windows was open a crack. Tuck eased over to the window and looked inside through the sheer curtains. Just as he decided to open the window the rest of the way and step in, Lucy, the private security guard stepped into the room. It was now or never. Tuck quickly and almost silently stuck one of the darts in her jugular vein and watched her twitch once and then fall to the floor in a heap. He stepped quickly into the room and retrieved his dart and her pistol. Tuck also took her radio and turned it off before placing it under the cushion of a love seat that was beside her.

Moving quickly now, he made his way to Milton's study where they had talked to him that afternoon, but Milton wasn't there.

"Looking for me, Maynard?" Milt's voice came from behind Tuck.

Tuck raised his arms up and turned slowly, expecting to be shot at any second. As he faced Milton Bunch, the man's eyes glass over and he fell to the floor like a sack of potatoes. There in the side of his neck was one of Shaun's darts, and there just behind him was Shaun with a big grin on his face. They quickly each got an arm and dragged Milt's limp and heavy body outside and to the SUV at almost a run, throwing him in the back seat where Tuck followed. Shaun jumped in the driver's seat and they were soon moving slowly back to 25E South and the rendezvous with the Interpol contact.

"That was great work, Tuck, although I thought old Milton had you for a second," Shaun told him.

"Yeah, I thought he did too. What kept you?" Tuck asked.

"I ran into Agnes coming out of the bathroom. After putting her to sleep, I saw her purse on a side table so I got my thousand bucks back," Shaun explained, "I got to thinking about my fingerprints on the money and realized that probably wasn't the smartest thing that I'd ever done."

"Well, we didn't have to kill anyone tonight, which is a plus for me. How long before that sleep agent wears off?" Tuck asked as he zip tied Milt's arms and legs, duct taped his mouth, and then climbed over the seat and back into the front of the SUV.

"Well, that's the thing. I've never tried that one before so I wasn't real sure about the dosage. They should be all right in maybe ten to twelve hours," Shaun answered.

"But not dead, right?" Tuck pressed.

"No, definitely not dead," Shaun reassured him as they drove the speed limit up route 11 and over to I-75 and to the Knoxville airport.

## CHAPTER 25

As soon as Susy Ellis heard the news that Daniel had been arrested, she went to the jail to see him, but his situation made that visit impossible.

"Missus Ellis, I'm sorry ma'am, but the sheriff is not in his right mind. We had to have six men bring him in here from the car, and he is still very unstable," the jailer told her.

"I really need to see him, is there not any way that I can at least look at him and make sure he's all right?" she asked.

"We've got him in an isolated unit, ma'am. If you will promise not to call out to him, I'll take you back there and let you see what we are up against," he replied.

They made their way back to the isolation cell where Daniel was still in restraints. He was pacing and mumbling incoherently to others that were not in the room. Susy couldn't bear to look at him that way so she just nodded to the jailer who took her arm and helped her back to the front.

"Has anyone looked at him to check his health?" she asked.

"I think that they have an arraignment scheduled for this afternoon, if I were you, I'd be there with a lawyer. A good lawyer might get him sent to a hospital for evaluation, but you didn't hear that from me," he replied.

Susy just nodded and left the building feeling like the weight of the world had fallen on her. This seemed to all start when she lost her job and the bills started piling up. Daniel started coming up with fantastic schemes to make extra money, and now he was in jail and facing serious prison time. She was at wits end when her name was mentioned.

"Hello, Missus Ellis," a young man walking with a much older silver haired man that must have been his grandfather had spoken to her.

"Hello…I don't think that we've met," she replied, shading her eyes from the sun which was behind him.

"It's Jimmy Johnson, Ma'am, you were at a tea that mom had last year," he said.

"Why yes, Jimmy, you're Ruth Ann's son. I am so glad that you weren't killed by those animals, and I'll bet that your mother is also," she told him.

"Missus Ellis, this is Pastor Josiah Perkins. He is taking me to a juvenile hearing in a little while. We heard about Sheriff Daniel and I wanted you to know how sorry I am. I should never have told him about the silver cave," Jimmy spilled out.

Susy started crying and Josiah took her by the arm and led her to a bench seat that was on the sidewalk in front of The Flocoe.

"Jimmy, how about going inside and getting us a couple of drinks, cold water for me. What would you like, Missus Ellis?" he asked.

"I'm fine Pastor Perkins. I just need to find a good lawyer to help my husband, but there isn't any money to pay one," Susy told him.

"Why don't we let God find that lawyer for you, Ma'am? Are you a praying woman?" he asked.

"I'm afraid not in years, sir. I'm almost ashamed to ask God for anything since it has been so long," she replied with her head down.

"Nonsense, God isn't at all concerned with that right now. I'm going to pray for you and your husband, and I'm expecting God to show up," Josiah told her.

He took her hand and bowed his head, praying to the God of the universe for an intercession in Susy and Daniel's lives. As soon as he was through, he reached into his pocket and took out a tract with a one hundred dollar bill and handed it to her. She just looked at it and shook her head.

"I can't take that money from you, Pastor Perkins. It just wouldn't be right," she told him.

"I get blessed by being a blessing. Now take the money so I can get my blessing, and if you need someone to talk to, my number is on the tract," he said with a big smile.

Susy was thanking him when her phone rang in her purse, "Excuse me, Pastor. Hello. Yes, this is Susy Ellis. Why yes I am. You would? That is too good to be true. I'll meet you at the courthouse for the hearing. Thank you so much!"

"Good news?" Josiah asked.

"That was from one of our most prestigious law firms and they want to handle Daniel's defense pro bono. Can you believe that?" she replied.

"Praise the Lord!" Josiah said with a smile.

Jimmy came out with the drinks as Susy was getting ready to go to the courthouse, so they all walked together with Josiah gently explaining to Susy how faith works. They waited for an hour before the courtroom opened and shortly afterward, an attorney showed up to represent Daniel Ellis. Susy went into a conference room with him and left Jimmy and Josiah to wait by themselves. The court heard Jimmy's case first and found him guilty of several misdemeanors. He was remanded into his Mother's custody and given 90 days of community service.

"Pastor Perkins, I want to thank you for speaking up for my boy," Ruth Ann Johnson told him when they had stepped out of the courtroom.

"It was my pleasure, Missus Johnson. If the family needs anything, please call me again," he told her, "I'm going back in to see what the outcome of the sheriff's arraignment is going to be."

Daniel was brought out muttering and disheveled with his wrists and his legs shackled to the wheelchair. Susy was in tears seeing him like this, but Josiah recognized the problem, especially when the demon possessed man turned to look in his direction and gave him an evil smile with his eyes flashing a red glow momentarily when they met his gaze. After arguments on both sides, the judge ordered that Daniel be transferred to the Mountain Home Veterans Administration Clinic in Knoxville for a thorough evaluation of his competency, and then the court was recessed. Josiah made the drive back to Knoxville with an uneasy feeling in his spirit that he hadn't seen the last of Daniel Ellis.

Joe Cloud sat for a few minutes in his truck after the other fish and game people had finished hunting down the last of the two big boars that had escaped from the rifle fire of earlier in the morning. He was still in a state of shock over what he had seen, although his father had not been slack in his teachings of Joe when he was a young boy in spiritual matters, but demons in the twenty-first century, come on. Joe always wrote those stories off to preachers trying to scare folks into church, but not anymore. He decided to run into Pineville and hit the McDonald's for a late lunch just to get out of the woods for a while. Tonight he would call home and talk to his father, but right now a fish sandwich and a Coke seemed to be the most important thing to do.

Joe turned the truck around and took a long look at the spot where they found the deputies head before leaving.

As he was heading in, his cell phone rang, "Joe, we need for you to meet a group of University of Kentucky Archeologists and take them out to that spot where the Swift cave is supposed to be. The Johnson boy is going along as part of his community service."

"You're kidding me, right? After what has gone on out here in the last few days, some egg head wants to dig up that cave?" Joe asked.

"Afraid so, Joe. Where do you want to meet them?" his boss asked.

"I'm heading to the McDonald's for lunch. How about sending them over there and they can follow me back out, but just for the record, I think this is a very bad idea," he replied.

"Noted, Joe, I'll send them along," the call ended.

Joe just shook his head and drove on to the McDonald's. Maybe he could get his food down before they showed up. That, however, was not to be. As soon as he parked, the 1956 Chevy of Jimmy Johnson showed up and parked beside him followed closely by the U of K official SUV loaded with gear, a trailer with two four wheelers, and two men, one obviously a professor, the other his younger assistant.

Joe just sat still for a second and closed his eyes. Sometimes making a quick stop in his 'Happy Place' calmed his nerves, but not today. Joe breathed a sigh and got out of the truck.

"Officer Cloud? We are with the University of Kentucky's Archeological department, I'm Doctor James Elkton and this is my assistant Dan Treat," The taller of the two extended his hand.

Joe nodded to them, "Let's get in out of this heat folks, I'm starving."

Joe knew Jimmy from some other dealings with the boy, mostly minor offenses, but the parents had always gotten him off.

"Hello, Officer Cloud," Jimmy greeted him.

"Hello Mister Johnson, Are you going to stay out there on this dig or just giving them directions," Joe asked as they entered the restaurant.

"Just giving directions, sir. I really don't want to go back out there after what happened," Jimmy told him.

Joe noticed that the young man was acting differently like he had lost the punk attitude that kept him in so much trouble. They ordered and found a table before Joe asked Jimmy to tell him about that ordeal.

"Well, you know that I found the cave while I was hunting last year, kind of by accident. When I found that silver in it, I told the sheriff because I didn't know what to do with it. Sheriff Ellis came up with the idea for me to disappear so we could work around the clock with the help of his two deputies getting that silver out of there. None of us knew about the hogs then. That night when Johnny Simpson brought out the sacks for us to start hauling the silver out was the first time that I had seen any sign of them over there, and they attacked us so fast that there was nothing that I could do to help him. I tried to carry him to the boat, but he was hurt too bad so I had to leave him," the boy told his story with the archeologists listening intently.

"Well, we killed all of those hogs this morning," Joe told him, "and I think that someone else might have shanghaied your silver folks. A logging helicopter made a pickup over there this morning."

"Well, it is not about the silver for us, Officer Cloud, we want to excavate the cave and collect any artifact from the seventeen hundreds that might be in there. Jimmy said there were tools and molds and such that were in a pile back in the cave. This could be a huge find for us," the professor told him.

"Well, let's get out there and you can get started working. Have you got a room in town?" Joe asked.

"No, we generally just pitch a tent near the dig and stay there until we are finished. There will be a few more helpers showing up in two days after we get the opening cleared," the professor told him.

The thought of spending any time out there made Joe's neck hair raise, much less sleeping in a tent on the ground.

"Do you men have any firearms with you for personal protection?" Joe asked.

"We don't believe in owning firearms, officer. I've been all around the world and have never had the need for one," the professor sounded self-righteous.

Jimmy caught Joe's eye and gave a little sideways shake of his head. It was apparent to Joe that whatever had happened out there at the cave that night had made a new man out of Jimmy Johnson.

"Well, let's get this show on the road. Jimmy and I will go in with you and help set up camp," Joe told them.

They finished eating and headed back out to the cannon Creek Lake and the Swift cave. Jimmy left the Chevy at the McDonald's and rode with Joe. When they reached the end of George Tuttle road, they helped Dan and Doctor Elkton get their gear packed onto the Polaris Ranger four wheelers that they had brought along.

"Well, Jimmy, why don't you and Dan lead the way. We'll follow you in," Joe told him.

The two-mile trip in was slow and rough until they found a trail that ran close to the lake. Dan opened up the Polaris a bit and they bounced along at a good pace, arriving about three hours before dark. After setting up the tents as close to where Jimmy indicated that the cave mouth was, Joe made home a fire pit with the warning to keep everything in and don't take a chance on burning down the woods.

"Doctor Elkton, I'm going to borrow one of your ATVs and that trailer if you don't mind. I wouldn't want to leave anything out here for the vultures to steal if you know what I mean," Joe told him.

"Be our guest Officer Cloud. Will you be back in the morning? I think we will probably wait until then to start opening the cave back up," Elkton asked.

"No, I think that I'll probably come out after lunch. We have a pretty good cell signal out here so if you need anything, give me a call and I can bring it out for you," Joe told them, Come on Jimmy, I want to get out of here before dark…so we don't get lost, you understand."

"Right behind you Officer Cloud," came the boy's reply.

"Are you sure that you want to stay out here tonight then?" Joe asked as he started the Polaris.

"We'll be fine, Officer, I've camped in lion country in Africa. Surely there's nothing here that is that dangerous," the doctor replied.

'Well, if you had asked me that yesterday at this time, I would have agreed with you, but I'm not so certain anymore," Joe said to the frowning professor as he drove away from the camp.

Jimmy leaned over closer to Joe so that he could talk over the noise of the engine, "Do I have to come back out here tomorrow?"

"I don't think so unless you want to. They told me that you were to just show them where the cave was," Joe answered.

"Good, I think if I live to be a hundred, I'm never coming out here again," Jimmy announced.

I don't blame you, kid. If I didn't have to be here, I'd find somewhere else where they hadn't heard of hogs or demons," Joe answered, "Did you tell those fellows the story about those hogs being demon possessed?"

"I mentioned it before we met you, but neither one of them believe in them…or in God for that matter," Jimmy replied.

Joe just shook his head and they finished the drive out without talking.

## CHAPTER 26

"Well, Doctor Elkton, do you want me to start pulling out some of those rocks that are blocking the cave entrance tonight?" Dan Treat asked.

"Dan, I'm concerned if we move too fast in this dig that we will miss some important artifacts. If you want to start pulling those larger stones out, just be careful not to disturb anything inside if we get through the blockage," Elkton told him.

"All right Doctor, I'm just anxious to get inside," Dan replied and started to work.

An hour later, the light was almost gone, and Elkton lit a Coleman gas lantern that illuminated the area around the tent.

"Professor, can you come over here? There is a smell of some kind here at the blockage," Dan called to him.

"I smell it too, Dan, what is it?" Elkton answered.

"When I was a kid, my uncle had a pig farm. That's what this reminds me of," he replied.

"Well that Johnson boy did say that the pigs they killed attacked them over here, I'll bet that smell is left over from them," Elkton replied and went back to his chair in front of the tent that he was staying in.

Dan moved a few more rocks and opened a hole about the size of a medium pumpkin in the middle of the cave opening. The smell that came out reeked of decay and hog offal, causing him to step backward in haste and vomit the evening MRE into the bushes.

"I can't do that anymore tonight, Doctor. The smell in there is unbelievable!" he exclaimed.

"Well, come on back over here and take a break. We'll attack it in the morning and be in there by ten," Doctor Elkton told him.

"You don't have to tell me twice on that, sir. Have you ever had one smell that badly before?" Dan asked as he opened a water to flush his mouth.

"No, just old and musty. This one is much worse. I'm going to turn in early, and I would suggest that you do the same. We have an early start tomorrow," Elkton told him.

"In a little while, Doctor. I'm going to text Kathy and tell her what we've been up to," Dan said

"Suit yourself," came the answer.

Just after midnight, the sound of a fist-sized rock rolling down the pile of debris at the entrance woke Dan from a deep sleep. He lay there for a minute trying to figure out what woke him when another rock dislodged and rolled down. Dan reached for his flashlight and unzipped the tent to have a look. When he shined his light over the cave mouth, it looked like the hole that he had made had grown to almost double in size, and for just a fleeting second, it appeared that something moved just inside.

Dan went closer, fighting the fear of the unknown that was rising in his mind, but he didn't see anything else.

"The rocks must have been loosened while I was working and slid down," he thought to himself, "At least there will be less smell in the morning if the hole is bigger."

Dan went back into the tent and climbed on the camping cot again. For a few minutes he just lay there with his eyes open, straining his ears for any sound that might come from the cave, but all that he heard was an owl far off and the mournful sound of a coyote across the lake.

The next sound that he heard two hours later was a blood-curdling scream coming from Elkton's tent. He grabbed his light, fumbled with the tent flap zipper that was caught for a minute in the fabric, and rushed outside to see Doctor Elkton's tent collapsed and several large shapes rolling around in the pile of fabric, one of which had to be the professor. The sound of a large rock moving caused Dan to swing his attention to the cave mouth just in time to see a very large hog that had managed to get his head through the opening but had gotten his shoulders stuck for the moment.

Another scream came from the tent, but it was weaker this time, and then suddenly it was gone. The only sounds now were the crunching noises coming from the tent, and the popping of the stuck hog's jaws as he fixated on Dan Treat who was frozen in fear. The hog thrashed violently and more rocks fell from the opening. Dan turned to run and remembered that he had forgotten his cell phone and boots in the tent.

There was no time for anything now but a panic-driven flight from the cave and into the woods toward the lake. Dan ran for his life down the hill somehow ignoring the pain of the sticks and rocks that were tearing at his feet. He could hear the hogs now coming out of the cave and tears started to well up behind his eyes at the thought that tonight would be his last one alive.

"DANNY, DANNY!" a man standing by a large old tree called to him.

Dan turned and ran toward the man that could barely be seen in the dim half light of a fading moon.

"Who are you?" he asked out of breath.

"Jeremiah, Danny. Now let me help you up this tree. Those hogs are right behind you. Get up in the fork and sit tight until morning. They can't get you up there," the man said.

"What about Doctor Elkton?" the boy asked as he climbed.

"He quit believing in me years ago, Danny. There is nothing that I can do for him," Jeremiah told him as he gave the boy's feet a shove that put him within reach of the large limbs.

Dan turned to asked him another question, but Jeremiah had gone, and a herd of ravenous hogs now encircled the tree.

## CHAPTER 27

Joe Cloud's phone rang at six the next morning just as he was thinking of catching another ten minutes sleep.

"Hello, Cloud speaking," he answered groggily.

"Officer Cloud, this is Professor Charlene Bixby from the University of Kentucky," a woman's voice answered, "I'm sorry to bother you this early, but Doctor Elkton gave me your phone number in case we couldn't reach him this morning."

"Go ahead, Professor Bixby, how can I help?" Joe asked.

"Well, we don't know how to get to the dig site, Officer Cloud. James was supposed to pick us up this morning and drive us in, but we are up here on George Tuttle road where his truck is parked and there is no sign of him," She answered.

"How many people did you bring, Professor? I've got one of the ATVs and can take three down to the cave," Joe told her, "but I wasn't due back until after noon."

"There are three of us, Officer. Can you come get us?" she asked.

"Sure, why not? I've got to get some coffee first if that's all right. Would you like for me to pick you up some?" he tried to be polite.

"Three black, Officer, and thank you," she replied.

"I'll be there in thirty minutes, ma'am," Joe ended the call and pulled on his trousers, he was starting to hate this job!

Thirty-five minutes later, Joe pulled up at the end of the road next to the blue Range Rover that Professor Bixby was driving. Standing by the front of her vehicle, Charlene Bixby cut quite a figure. An avid outdoors woman who like to hunt and fish, she was also without a doubt the most beautiful woman that Joe had ever seen. At five feet nine inches tall and one hundred and forty pounds, she was exactly the woman that Joe had always dreamed of, and her flaming red hair and green eyes were only icing on the cake to him.

"Professor Bixby?" Joe tried not to stutter.

"Hello, Officer Cloud, Charlene is fine," she said as she extended her hand.

"Joe is my name, Ma'am, you can call me Joe," he said quietly.

"Okay Joe, my girls are napping in the Rover. Let me wake them up and then I'll help you unload the ATV," she said as she took the coffee from him.

Joe started to work on the ATV straps and noticed that his hands were shaking. He made it through one side when Carlene came up and started the other.

"Cloud is Cherokee, isn't it?" she asked.

"It is, I'm full blooded Cherokee, Charlene," he answered hoping that didn't make a difference to her.

"We need to talk after I'm finished up here. My background is anthropology, and I am doing a paper on the Cherokee as one of the indigenous tribes of this area," she said while flashing a smile that made him forget what he was doing.

"I would be happy to Charlene. Perhaps you could meet my father who has the history of our people committed to memory," he told her, "but right now, I'm having trouble concentrating on the job at hand so we'll talk later."

She just gave him that big smile again as he rolled the Polaris off and started the engine. Joe walked over to his truck and grabbed the Remington 700 and a few rounds. After yesterday, he wasn't going into any woods without that rifle or one bigger in his hand.

"Why the rifle, Joe?" she asked.

"I don't know if you are aware, Charlene, but we had to kill some hogs out here yesterday that had killed a couple of men. I like to keep this old thing handy…just in case," he answered, "Get the girls loaded and we'll put their gear in the back."

Five minutes later, they were easing through the woods and trying not to spill the coffee. Joe was trying to catch a glimpse of Charlene at every opportunity only to find her doing the same with him while the two students in the back giggled.

When they finally arrived at the campsite, Joe was immediately aware that something was wrong. The tents were knocked down, and the ground was covered with bloody torn clothes.

"Stay in the vehicle, everyone!" he ordered.

Joe grabbed the rifle and threw a round in the chamber before walking slowly to the debris field in front of him. There was no sign of either Doctor Elkton or his sidekick, Dan. The tent fabric was torn and trampled as were the packs that the men were carrying, and there was a stench in the air that reminded him of death. Not the fresh kill kind, but the smell that came after something had died a few days before. Joe looked toward the cave and saw the now gaping hole in the mouth. He raised the rifle to his shoulder and eased over to look in, but the only evidence that something had been in there was the smell.

Joe walked back to the ATV where the frightened girls were blubbering in the back seat. Charlene looked cool as a cucumber in the front.

"What did you find?" she asked.

"Nothing, there is nothing alive over there. Lots of blood and the tents are torn up pretty badly, but there is no sign of Elkton or Dan," he told her, "Can you fire a rifle, Charlene?"

"Of course, I can, Joe," she replied.

"Good hold this and be ready for anything, I've got to call this in," he handed her the Remington.

Joe got on his cell phone and called in to his headquarters to ask for some backup and an ambulance just in case there was a survivor of the apparent hog attack.

"We should have some help out here in a bit, but I think that we should get back up to the road and wait there for it to arrive. Can you drive the other ATV?" he asked.

"Yes, I'll follow you, but we need to get out of here, I've got a bad feeling about this place, Joe," she said.

"Tell me about it," he replied, "Crank that up and let's see if it will run."

They made the trip back to the road in record time with the feeling that something was just behind them all of the way, but nothing showed. Thirty minutes later the place looked like a war zone triage center, complete with paramedics, state troopers, wildlife officers, and a CNN news crew. Joe talked to everyone including the CNN reporter, and gave directions to the emergency responders, most of whom had been on site the day before. Joe decided to stay with Charlene at the road command area until the cave site had been thoroughly swept for hogs and bodies. Well, at least the day hadn't been as bad as the past week had been, he mused as he watched the red hair of his dream girl blow in the soft summer breeze right next to him on the fender of the trailer where they were seated.

"Do you think that they are dead, Joe?" she asked quietly.

"I don't know really. There was enough blood for at least one of them to be dead, but there weren't any bodies," he said but failed to mention that hogs generally don't leave much behind.

Charlene wrote a note on a piece of paper and handed it to him, "Listen, I'm going to take the girls back to Lexington. There's really no use for us to stay here, and I'm sure not interested in the dig right now. Will you please give me a call tonight and let me know what's happening here?"

Joe's heart sank about three feet at the news that she was leaving, "Sure, I can do that."

"You know, Joe, Lexington isn't very far from here. You could come up and see me if you were inclined. We could talk about Cherokee history and stuff like that," Charlene told him with a smile as he walked her to the Range Rover.

"Well, I do clean up pretty good, Charlene. I'll call you tonight, and you can set a definite time for me to come up," he said with a smile.

Charlene smiled as she drove off back down George Tuttle road.

A half hour later, he heard the ATVs coming back out of the woods so he picked up the rifle and headed to meet them. In the front seat of the lead Polaris sat Dan Treat who looked to be in shock, but physically not injured.

Joe walked over to him as the medics were putting him in the ambulance, "Was it hogs, Dan?" he asked.

"Yes, hogs chased me down to the lake, but Jeremiah helped me up a tree. He said he couldn't help Doctor Elkton," the boy answered as if in a daze.

"Jeremiah?" Joe asked but got no response. That was the second time that he had heard the name in two days.

Joe nodded to the medics who shut the doors and left with the frightened kid. It had certainly been an interesting week. He started the Polaris and headed back down to the cave hoping that it was empty. The hogs that had attacked the professor and Dan needed to be trapped and put down, but those arrangements could be made later in the day. When he arrived at the cave, the area was sealed with yellow tape and the other law enforcement officers were talking by the cave mouth.

"Has anyone gone in yet?" Joe asked hopefully.

"The smell would run a vulture off of a gut wagon, Joe. None of us has the stomach for it," one of the troopers told him.

"Does anybody have a light?" Joe asked, "I'll wet a rag and tie it over my mouth and nose to keep some of it out. Who will go in with me?"

The men all looked at each other before one of the other wildlife officers spoke up.

"Why should you have all of the fun, Joe? Besides, we'll both be heroes after this gets on the news later," he said.

"Come on then, let's get this over with," Joe told him as he tied a towel that was in the wreckage of Dan's tent around his head.

The two stepped over the pile of broken rocks and entered the cave carefully. Joe had his Glock out and moved slowly into the depths of the cave trying not to gag. When the other officer had cleared the entrance, Joe turned and shined the light back at the rock wall behind them revealing a splashing of blood across the rocks that looked as if a madman with a pail has thrown it there. Looking down at the floor of the cave where the largest pieces of the ceiling had fallen, he saw Monroe's head and torso buried under the debris in a way that kept the hogs from eating that part of him, but the rest was gone. His partner threw his hand over his mouth and ran from the cave.

Joe turned back to shine the light further in, but the cave was empty as far back as he could see. He surmised that the low volume blast that he heard just before that helicopter got there yesterday was the sound of the cave being sealed with the bodies and the hogs still inside. This was the job for a medical examiner now so Joe turned and went back out into the daylight and fresh air.

He retrieved his rifle from the ATV and followed the hog tracks down to the cove, leaving the others to deal with the CNN reporters and the mess in the cave. It was evident that they had been worrying themselves around a tree that must have held Dan Treat until this morning. Joe worked his way closer to the lake and saw that the water in the shallow end of the cove was muddied up more than usual. He made a slow and careful stalk of the shoreline being careful to stop every few steps to listen, and then he heard a grunt coming from the muddied brush back from the water's edge about fifty yards from his position. He eased back out of the area and returned to the cave to round up some help. If they played their cards right, they had a good chance of killing most of this pack of hogs while they lay in their wallow.

Since most of the men had brought a rifle of some sort with them, and the troopers were carrying Colt M-4s, they devised a strategy that would have the men encircle the sleeping hogs and leave them only the water as an escape route. Joe would lead the team around the back of the cove while the troopers would take the side closest to the cave and shoot any hog that made it to the water. The CNN cameras would follow the troopers and were warned to keep quiet until the shooting started.

It took thirty minutes for the wildlife officers to work their way into position behind the sleeping hogs. Reminding themselves that these animals had killed and eaten men shortly beforehand kept them on their toes as they got their first look at the bedding animals. Joe shouldered his rifle as a sign to the men on his right and left, and then fired a round into the head of the nearest hog from a distance of twenty yards. The squealing of the frightened and wounded animals filled the air as the twelve hogs tried first to run left, and then to run away from the water's edge to no avail. The remaining five tried to swim across the narrow cove only to be met with the deadly fire of the troopers situated above them. Soon it was over, and the cove ran red with the blood of the animals that floated on its surface.

Leaving the others to finish the wounded animals and drag them out of the woods with the help of the ATVs, Joe walked back to the cave without reminding the celebrators that there were no sows or piglets in that group, and somewhere close, there was a whole new crop of pigs waiting to mature.

## CHAPTER 28

The prison transfer van pulled up to the emergency entrance to the Mountain Home V.A. Medical Center with Daniel Ellis. He had been heavily sedated and was in belly chains and leg irons for the trip even though he had been strapped in a wheelchair. The two guards that had transported him waited until they were joined by two orderlies before taking Daniel carefully out of the van and rolling him inside. Once the receiving paperwork had been signed, they breathed a sigh of relief and headed back to Pineville, Kentucky.

Daniel was rolled to an isolation ward and transferred to a hospital bed where his hands and feet were restrained to the bed rails. The transfer was without incident as he was extremely docile. Daniel opened his eyes the moment the orderlies had left the room and twisted his arms against the restraints with a supernatural strength until one of them broke. Although he had bruised his arm severely, Daniel felt no pain, only a deep and burning hatred and a desire to escape. Turel had found the perfect host for his band of demons this time, and now was the time to use it.

Within seconds, Daniel had loosed the straps on his other wrist and legs. He was still in the orange jumpsuit that he'd been transferred in and would need some clothes, but first came getting out of this place.

The door was locked but there was the sound of footsteps from the outside so he moved behind the door and turned off the lights. Shortly an orderly came into the room to run his blood work but ended up donating his clothes to Daniel's effort. He locked the naked and unconscious man in the bathroom and made his break out of the building following the exit signs. Nobody seemed to be concerned about the man with the crazy look in his eyes, partly because the simply didn't care. Knowing that it would only take a few minutes before he was missing, the possessed man made his way quickly to the least savory parts of the city so that he could blend in with many others that acted just like he did. Turel knew where he was going even if Daniel seemed lost and dazed. Revenge was at hand for the five years spent in the hog, and he would have that revenge if it took five more years to get it.

The news of Daniel's escape from the V.A. hospital reached Susy Ellis the next morning. She faulted herself for what Daniel had become simply because she thought that it was about the lack of household finances since she had lost her job that drove him to do the things that had brought him down. Susy wasn't a church goer by any stretch, but something about the kind old preacher that she had met touched her and made her feel less alone, something she had struggled with her whole life. Perhaps he could help, and the fact that he was in Knoxville where Daniel was couldn't hurt any. She contacted her sister down there and made arrangements to bring their mother for a visit.

Her next step was to call Josiah Perkins and tell him that she was coming and needed to see him. He told her where the little church was located and said that he would be glad to pray with her about Daniel, just call when she got to town. Feeling like a weight had been lifted from her, Susy packed the car and left Pineville.

"…and that was the last time I saw my Milty," Agnes Bunch told the FBI agent that was taking notes on his disappearance. Two other agents were questioning Lucy and Chester about what they saw, but both seemed less inclined to cooperate than Agnes, partly because of their lengthy rap sheets.

"Mrs. Bunch, I understand that you are upset, but have you got any idea who these men were?" the agent asked for the second or third time.

"Well, they did give Milty a business card. Now if I can just find it," she said and started rummaging through her purse," Here it is!"

The agent held the card with the Trade Winds Trading Company logo, "Was Bill Jackson the man that you remember?"

"Yes, that was it, and his son was named Maynard," she responded.

"Okay, Ma'am, I've got everything that I need. We'll be in touch if we have any developments," he told her as he got up and nodded to the others.

When they got outside one of them asked, "What did you find out?"

He just handed the business card over, "Take a look at this."

"Oh crap, if Trade Winds is involved, we'd better not be. Is that what you're thinking, Steve?" he asked after looking at the card.

"I think we need to stop by The Flocoe on the way out and get some coffee and a bite. Somebody higher up the totem needs to deal with this case," the agent 'Steve' told them, "This is likely an Interpol operation, and I wouldn't want to bungle it up."

"What would Interpol want with that old man?" the other agent asked.

Steve turned to them as they were getting in the car and said, "I don't even want to know. When we get back, we need to run a check on those other two, though. Now who's buying?"

The next week flew by like a rocket, and life in Pineville gradually returned to normal, or as normal as it could get. Jimmy Johnson showed up at the First Baptist Church on Sunday accompanied by his mother, Ruth Ann, and both Doris and Emily Hobbs. He sat in the front trying to ignore the finger pointing and whispers until Pastor Timothy gave the altar call, and Jimmy went down and knelt before the Lord.

Susy Ellis was in church at the New Bethel Fellowship pastored by Josiah Perkins that Sunday and cried through the entire service. A group of woman gathered around her during the altar call and prayed with the distraught woman. She had been raised in the Primitive Baptist tradition and had never felt the love that was present in this little place. For the first time in her life, Susy Ellis had her hope renewed like the first rays of a warm sun after a hard winter.

Bob and Abigail Pike flew to Barbados with Tuck, Hanna, and the children instead of returning immediately to La Ceiba. The warm sunshine and the gentle trade breeze did much to wash away the horrors of the previous week, and the grief of the past two years.

Joe Cloud and his father drove to Lexington, Kentucky on Saturday to spend the day with Charlene Bixby. Charlene stole the old man's heart as much as she had Joe's by the end of the day. Although Joe had thought to take Charlene to dinner, she insisted on cooking for them herself. After an evening that passed too quickly, Joe and his father retired to the Hampton Inn room that they had rented so they could be with Charlene in church the following morning.

"I like this one, Joe," his father told him, "You need to marry her."

"Geez, Dad, I just met her this week," Joe gave a half-hearted protest.

"All the same, this is the woman that God has sent you, and I need grandchildren," his father laughed.

Joe couldn't help but think how much life could change in just a few short days.


In a dark and seedy section of Knoxville, the old man exited the back of the storefront church that he had founded many years before. The Wednesday night service following the fellowship meal had been good with three young people getting saved, and Josiah Perkins gave thanks as he walked the short distance to his old car that sat in the alley behind the building. The rest of his parishioners had gone home an hour before, leaving him alone to lock the church and turn out the lights.

As he walked slowly across the alley behind the strip mall, Josiah noticed a man coming toward him with an unsteady gate. Judging from his unkempt appearance, it seemed as if this was another homeless person looking for a handout, which the old preacher was never reluctant to give along with a gospel tract and a kind word.

When the man drew closer to him, however, Josiah noticed that there was something wrong with the eyes that appeared to be fixated on him and nothing else.

"Josiah Perkins!" came a voice that fell between a shriek and a cackle on the pastor's ears.

"I'm Josiah Perkins," replied the preacher, "What can I do for you?"

"I've looked for you a long time, ever since you were up in Pineville meddling in affairs that did not concern you," he answered.

Inside, the old preacher felt a stirring that could only be a warning from the Holy Spirit.

"I didn't get your name, friend," Josiah replied calmly.

"My name is LEGION!" shouted the man.

"Ah, I've been looking for you, Turel," Josiah told him.

Suddenly, the alley was lit by a brilliant white light, as the figure of the old man was replaced by a nine-foot tall being of light.

"Raphael!" the man shrieked in terror with what sounded like several hundred voices.

"Back to the abyss with you, Turel, and all of your minions!" the angel Raphael ordered, "You will remain there under shards of sharp rock until the return of the Lord and His judgment!"

The light dimmed in the alley as suddenly as it came and the man collapsed in a sobbing heap to the dirty pavement.

Josiah Perkins knelt beside the young man and cradled his head in his arms.

"Are you all right, friend?" he asked.

"I feel like I've been cleaned up and set free," the man answered, "Things have been so wrong for so long. I've made a real mess of things."

"Come on inside, son, I'll put us some coffee on and heat up the leftovers from dinner," Josiah gently helped him to his feet and walked him back to the church, "What do I call you?" although he knew who he was.

"Daniel, sir, Daniel Ellis. I used to be the sheriff up in Bell County Kentucky," he replied, "I need to turn myself in."

"There's no hurry, Daniel, you can do that later. By the way, I have a young woman in my flock named Susy Ellis, any relation?" Josiah asked knowingly, "She's been praying mighty hard for her husband."

## CHAPTER 29

Tom Strongbow was amazed at the brightness of the early summer colors in the Pee Dee swampland as he rode his Kawasaki four-wheeler along the three-mile tract of land that his hunting lodge had recently leased to expand their range down the river bottom. The blue birds were an exotic crisp blue, and the finches exhibited an amazing brightness to their yellow colors, as did the occasional cardinal that passed by. Even the trees had a special sharpness to the outline of their leaves that he had not noticed on the many other trips that he made into the swamp as he took a personal responsibility for his client's welfare and success.

Today the rifle had been left in the truck while he checked his trail cams for footage of the hogs and deer that he expected to start hunting in the next couple of months as soon as he and his helpers could get all of their stands and blinds set up to give the hunters the best advantage.

Tom gave little thought to the experience with the killer hogs in Pineville now that he was back on familiar soil. The truth of it was that except for the demon spirits in that pack, there was very little difference in the behavior of hogs anywhere. They had always been a dangerous animal to hunt, and they would eat anything that was put in front of them, animal, vegetable, or human. The demon aspect just iced the cake so to speak.

At the far end of the property, Tom stopped to check his feeder, a four-foot piece of PVC pipe with holes drilled in it to let the corn slowly out, and the ends capped. Corn kernels were placed in the pipe, and then the end was screwed on before the pipe was chained to a steel stake. The hogs would roll the pipe to and fro, shaking the corn out in small amounts, but they couldn't get it all at one time. Today the pipe was missing and the steel stake that had been its tether had been bent at right angles to the ground.

As he looked at the size of the tracks around where the feeder had been, the hair on his neck began to stand up and anxiety began to build. Tom walked quietly toward the swamp edge and saw the feeder pipe floating in the shallow water, but it was not alone. Raising itself up like a king Cobra, a huge Cottonmouth moccasin turned his head to stare with is red glowing eyes directly at Tom and his knees buckled.

Tom realized that somehow he had let the time get past him, and now it was starting to get dark in this area of the swamp. The feeling of fear was taking a strong hold on him as he made his way back to the Kawasaki and turned the key. Nothing happened. The battery was as dead as a doornail. He pulled his cell phone out of his pocket and tried to call the lodge for help, although that would take an hour or more to reach him. No service was available.

There was now a palpable chill in the air now as if a storm was blowing in, but the sky was still clear. Somehow, he needed to move away from this spot, but fear had mired his feet to the sodden ground, and Tom was having trouble walking. He knew that he needed to pray, but his voice wouldn't work. The double seat ladder stand was directly in front of him so he decided to climb that rather than stay on the ground. As he tried to get his feet onto the lower rung, a noise like something heavy coming through the woods caught his ear, and his panicked feet refused to climb.

Tom turned slowly to face whatever was making that sound. Suddenly from the underbrush a very large hog with glowing red eyes appeared and looked right at him.

"Tommy, Tommy, RUN," a voice screamed at him but he couldn't see it.

"I can't move!" he almost couldn't make the sound as the hog came closer.

"Tom, Tom, wake up!" he heard Angie call to him.

Tom lay on his back covered in sweat with his heart racing so hard that his chest hurt.

"Tom, what in the world were you dreaming about?" Angie asked.

"Just a bad dream, I guess, Hon. What time is it?" he asked.

"Just after six. Do you have to get up early today? We just got back." she asked concerned.

"Yeah, I've got to check on the new tract of land that we leased." He answered as he got out of bed, "go back to sleep."

Tom turned on the coffee pot and did his morning devotions while the coffee brewed. He turned the television on just in time to catch the tail end of the CNN newscast.

"My oh my, what is going on in Pineville, Kentucky? A few days ago we reported ex-senator Andrew Trent found murdered in his office, and then we reported the disappearance of one of his staunchest foes, Milton Bunch, a retired businessman. Now just look what else is happening close by. There is still no word on the outcome of the search that has been underway for one the two men that disappeared yesterday while working near Pineville, Kentucky. The men were part of an archeological team that has been excavating an old cave near the city reservoir where it was rumored that Jonathon Swift may have cast silver ingots during the mid-seventeen hundreds. Authorities have only found the bloody remains of the tents and the backpacks that the men were to be carrying plus a few torn pieces of clothing. Our camera crew was on the scene when the searchers shot a herd of hogs that may have been the culprits. Warning, this video has some violent scenes so send your children out of the room."

Tom turned off the television and headed back to the bedroom, "I changed my mind, Angie. The property can wait."

# ACKNOWLEDGEMENTS

I would like to thank Tom Naumann, owner of the Cherokee Run Hunting Lodge LLC for lending his professional hunting wisdom for technical support and also for his strong Christian influence over the years, which helped me to shape the character of Tom Strongbow for this novel. For those of you, that would like to visit his website: http://www.eatsleephunt.com

Also, I would like to thank the many establishments that are mentioned in this work of fiction to give it a feel of realism.

## OTHER BOOKS BY W.W.BROCK:

COUGAR!

NIGHT WIND

THUNDER RANCH

TEXAS RISING